CONTENTS

CORGI CASE FILES

Case of the
Great Cranberry Caper

Corgi Case Files, Book 11

J.M. Poole

Sign up for Jeffrey's newsletter on his
website to get all the latest corgi news:
www.AuthorJMPoole.com

Case of the Great Cranberry Caper
Published by Secret Staircase Books, an imprint of
Columbine Publishing Group, LLC
PO Box 416, Angel Fire, NM 87710

This book is a work of fiction. Names, characters, places and incidents
are either the product of the author's imagination or are used
fictitiously. Any resemblance to actual events or locales or persons, living
or dead, is entirely coincidental. Although the author and publisher
have made every effort to ensure the accuracy and completeness
of information contained in this book we assume no responsibility
for errors, inaccuracies, omissions, or any inconsistency herein. Any
slights of people, places or organizations are unintentional.

Book layout and design by Secret Staircase Books
Cover images © Elena Yakinova, Irina Miroschnichenko, Naddiya, Stephen
Dumayne, Anna Rudenko, Yevgen Kacharin, and the image of the tri-
color corgi is courtesy of Jeffrey Poole and Kinsey the cover dog!

First trade paperback edition: November 2020
First e-book edition: November 2020

* * *

Publisher's Cataloging-in-Publication Data

Poole, J.M.
Case of the Great Cranberry Caper / by J.M. Poole.
p. cm.
ISBN 978-1649140418 (paperback)
ISBN 978-1649140425 (e-book)

1. Zachary Anderson (Fictitious character)--Fiction. 2.
Pomme Valley, Oregon (fictitious location)—Fiction. 3. Amateur
sleuth—Fiction. 4. Pet detectives—Fiction. I. Title

Corgi Case Files Mystery Series : Book 11.
Poole, J.M., Corgi Case Files mysteries.

BISAC : FICTION / Mystery & Detective.
813/.54

ACKNOWLEDGMENTS

This will mark the first novel released by my new publisher, Secret Staircase Books, an imprint of Columbine Publishing Group. Many thanks to them for giving this (former) indie author a try!

As always, I need to give thanks to my Posse. You know who you are, and what you've done for me. You guys are the best! Diane, Elizabeth, Mefe, Jason, Louise and Caryl. Thanks for taking time out of your busy day to give me a hand.

I hope you enjoy the story! Happy reading!

This book is dedicated to the readers.

*Stay safe in this crazy world and, whatever you do,
mask up until this pandemic is under control.*

PROLOGUE

W hat did you say it was called, again?" a hesitant voice asked. "Carbonocity, er, carbon...?"

"A carbonaceous chondrite," another voice answered. "Pay attention, would you?"

"I am! That sounds very specific. And, um, what is that, exactly?"

"Oh, for heaven's sake," the second voice grumbled. "You should know about these things by now."

"Just pretend for a second that I don't," the first voice argued. "Can't you just tell me what it is?"

"A carbonaceous chondrite," Second Voice sighed, as though he had been asked this very question numerous times, "is very primitive. Its chemical composition more closely matches the sun than any other type of chondrite. With me so far?"

"Uh, sure."

"The thing to remember," Second Voice continued, as he ignored the sarcastic response from his companion, "is that there are different clans and groups of chondrites. Not all are the same, but you already know this, don't you?"

"You don't have to get snarky."

"You don't have a clue what I'm talking about, do you? How did you ever manage to get hired on here as an intern?"

"I like the stars, okay? Be nice to me."

"Or, what? Are you going to tattle to your mother?"

"Stop treating me like I'm a child."

"Then, stop acting like one. Now, are you finished complaining? Are you ready to get to work?"

"Sure, I guess. Where's Professor Owens?"

Second Voice grunted, "He'll be back soon."

"Do you need me to get it?"

"I already have it," Second Voice pointed out. "Besides, you aren't supposed to be messing with his desk, not without direct supervision."

"Hey, I may be an intern, but I can be trusted."

"Mm-hmm. Sure, you can. Have you seen it yet?"

"Hmm? Oh, you're talking about the ...? No, I haven't."

"Want a look at where the host came from?"

The man adjusting the controls on the bank of electronics put his hands in his pockets and stepped away from the counter. Only when the young intern was sitting at the Con, as the observatory staff had jokingly named the huge telescope's command seat, did a smile appear on the young kid's face. He looked deferentially at his companion, who nodded permission, before placing a hand on a bank of controls and making a few adjustments.

The image on the screen sharpened and intensified. A sea of polychromatic pinpricks leapt into focus. A pale green rectangle suddenly appeared on the upper right quadrant. The screen blurred out as the computer redrew the night sky in the selected area. A few more minutes of fine-tuning the image brought a very familiar image to the screen.

"There you go," Second Voice said, from behind the command chair. "Based on its trajectory, this baby originated in the Andromeda Galaxy. Now, look over here. See the monitor? I currently have a tiny slice in the magnifier. Now, do you see that? Those striations right there should be able to identify some of the minerals comprising this specimen."

"Umm ..."

"Don't overthink it," Second Voice instructed. "Just ..."

A loud beeping startled them both. Second Voice hastily retrieved his cell and glanced at the display. Reading the text message which had popped up on the display, he groaned.

"Everything okay?"

"Professor Owens is back on campus. He's demanding a meeting with all department heads."

"Ugh. When?"

"In 30 minutes. We'd best start wrapping up here."

The intern hastily vacated the Con while Second Voice took over. Expertly punching buttons and twisting knobs, the giant telescope, and all its accompanying devices and peripherals, including the digital high-res magnifier, powered down. Snapping on a pair of latex gloves, Second Voice retrieved the sample from the magnifier and studied it up close. Then, catching sight of a glittering object sitting unobtrusively near the monitor, Second Voice tsked to himself.

"What is it?" First Voice asked.

"Professor Owens would be *beside* himself if he knew this had been left out," Second Voice breathed. "Heads would *roll*."

"I could put it away for you. It goes in the Professor's desk, doesn't it?"

"It does, but I'll do it. It's very rare."

"What do you know about it?" First Voice asked.

"Well, I can tell you that it's not from around here. This was found inside NB414."

"That? That was inside NB414?"

"Well, it didn't look like this. Someone decided to get it cut and polished."

"Wow. Do they all have something like that in them?" First Voice asked. "I never would have likened them to oysters."

Second Voice shrugged. "That's what we're doing: analyzing. Once we identify all the compounds, then we can get a better idea of where it came from, what it has seen, and so on."

"How often do they contain those things?" First Voice asked.

"As you may, or may not, be able to tell, specimens this size are exceedingly rare."

"Where did this one strike? Does anyone know? Northern or Southern hemisphere?"

"Northern," Second Voice answered.

"Where?" the intern pressed.

"One of the Canadian provinces. New Brunswick, hence the 'NB' of its name."

"Oh. I just now got that."

"Make sure your station is powered down," Second Voice ordered. "The Prof wants to meet with us in the conference room. We can't leave everything out in the open like this."

A second round of angry beeping occurred. Once more, Second Voice fished his phone out of his pocket and glanced at the display. This time, he stifled a curse.

"It's Professor Owens. I have to take this."

"Go. I can finish here. We don't want the Prof to be mad at us. He has a temper."

"Don't I know it. Are you sure?"

"Of course. I'll see you guys in the conference room."

Now that he was alone, the intern began to whistle while he started shutting off the smaller pieces of electronic equipment. Computers, printers, and microscopes were deactivated, one by one, as the intern moved from station to station. Coming full circle back to the Con, his eyes fell on the digital magnifier and what was still on it. His eyes shot open with surprise.

Had his companion, Professor Owen's favorite grad student, been distracted by the call?

Holding the object up to the nearest light, the intern suddenly smiled as a thought came to him. He snatched up the object and hurried out of the observatory, stopping only long enough to secure the telescope room.

He had made it all the way to the observatory's front entrance before an alarm began to wail. Who had sounded the alarm? How could they have discovered it was missing so quickly? The only explanation was that someone had stopped back by the professor's office. Someone must have decided he was untrustworthy. Then again, to their credit, he *did* just steal the blasted thing. However, this wasn't planned. He hadn't woken up this morning with the intent on stealing anything from anybody.

It was just *there*, waiting to be taken.

Stifling a curse, the intern looked down at the object clutched tightly in his hand and moaned. Perhaps this wasn't such a good idea after all? What was he going to do?

He knew full well that, if he should be caught with this particular specimen in his possession, then his career would be ruined. More than likely, it meant he would be looking at possible incarceration for life. He had to hide it, but the question was, where? Where could he stash this blasted thing so that he could collect it at a later date?

Sirens sounded in the distance. Frantic and desperate, the young intern scanned his immediate surroundings, hoping an idea would come. There had to be somewhere he could stash this thing. Where could he put it so that he could reclaim it at a later date?

As luck would have it, a solution presented itself in remarkable time. The intern began to run.

ONE

Nothing in this beautiful world of ours could possibly compare to the majesty of the Pacific Northwest during autumn. That's in my own humble opinion, of course. Add on the fact that it was the first week of November, and my fiancée and I were strolling—hand-in-hand—through Cider Fest, a harvest festival which lasted several months, and I could easily believe I was in paradise.

For those of you who may not know me, allow me to introduce myself. My name is Zachary Anderson, although my friends call me Zack. I live in picturesque Pomme Valley, Oregon, which is located in the southwestern area of the state. We're about twenty miles west of Medford, and a little under thirty miles to the east of Grants Pass.

Now, many of you are probably not familiar enough with our fair state to know where that's at, let alone having even heard of Pomme Valley. What I can tell you is that we're pretty much at the bottom of the state, while directly above us

... make that over 400 miles directly above us, is Portland. PV (as the locals call it) is barely a blip on the map, with a population of less than 3,000, yet during the last two months of the year, our population can easily triple—or quadruple— on the weekends. That was why it was practically standing room only at the merchant stalls. Everyone wanted to be outside, enjoying the weather. Everyone wanted to get into the spirit of the upcoming holidays.

Poor Sherlock and Watson had to resort to ... look at that. I'm getting ahead of myself again. Alrighty, let's fix that. I need to finish the intros. You know who I am, so let me introduce my fiancée, Jillian. Jillian Cooper, age *classified*, is the owner of Cookbook Nook and probably the wealthiest woman living on the West Coast. Much to her credit, she doesn't flaunt her wealth, or throw it in peoples' faces. Much the opposite. Jillian took it upon herself to help her friends open their own businesses, while acting like a silent partner. Even she doesn't know how many companies she has had a hand in starting up.

Before I go any further, I feel I should set the record straight. If you think I'm only with Jillian because of her financial status, then think again. I may not be as loaded as she is, but my own financial security is better than most. Not only am I a successful romance novelist, but the private winery that I own is bringing in a hefty profit, too. In fact, there have been a few months where the wine sales have exceeded book sales, which isn't an easy feat.

As if those two sets of responsibilities weren't enough to keep me busy, I held down a third job: police consultant. Thankfully, the third job really doesn't require me to do too much. You see, that would fall to my two dogs, Sherlock and Watson.

Just like their namesakes, my two dogs solve crimes. Don't laugh, I'm serious. Those two corgis are capable of ... hey, I said no laughing! And yes, you heard right. Sherlock and Watson are corgis. They are, without a doubt, some of the most unintimidating looking dogs I have ever encountered. However, they are also some of the smartest. What can I say? Here, in PV, my dogs are very well known.

Let me give you a few examples.

For starters, Sherlock kept my rear out of jail when I first moved here. The police thought I had committed a murder and, thankfully it was proven without a shadow of a doubt that I couldn't have been responsible. Oh, let's see. What's another good example? Well, how about tracking down the guy responsible for stealing presents at Christmas? Or discovering who was responsible for the death of a well-known SCUBA diver while we were vacationing in Monterey, CA?

Trust me, the list goes on and on. I can't even begin to imagine how the dogs are able to do it. Somehow, and I've never been able to determine how, whenever we're working a case, or are assisting Vance with one of his, Sherlock and Watson will inevitably be drawn to *something* that appears to be unrelated. After the case has been solved, however, and we start reviewing all our 'corgi clues', as we call them, then we can see that the dogs were easily two steps ahead of us at all times.

How? How do they do it? How could they know a passing car is being driven by a murder suspect? How do they know a dog-napped cocker spaniel was being held in the root cellar of a house they've never seen before?

The list goes on and on. As many times as I say that I'm determined to figure out the significance of the corgi clues before the case is over, I have yet to do so. At least I can say that I'm not the only one who is (clearly) slow on the uptake. Vance and I have wasted countless hours poring through photographs, or revisiting locales in town where the dogs have expressed interest, or ...

Look at that. I just realized I had forgotten someone.

Vance Samuelson is a very good friend of mine who happens to live here, in PV. He's a detective on the police force and is the one responsible for bringing me and the dogs in on cases whenever he needs a helping hand. Or paw. Vance is married to a woman by the name of Tori, who's a teacher at the local high school. She's incredibly intelligent, funny, and someone not to cross if she, or anyone in her family, is threatened in any way, shape, or form. Vance and Tori have two daughters, Victoria and Tiffany.

So, yes, you could say I lead an idyllic life in my little town here in the great state of Oregon. Life was good, it was treating me well, and I can't complain. If you would have known me a few years ago, you would know that my life, then, was nowhere close to the Utopia I was in now.

A little over two years ago, I was married to a wonderful woman by the name of Samantha Masters. She was my high school sweetheart, and we enjoyed a little over twenty years together. That, unfortunately, came to a screeching halt when Samantha was killed in a head-on collision in what I had thought was an accident, only it was proved—later—to be premeditated murder. Thankfully, that painful story has already been told, and I don't need to tell it again.

So, why bring it up? It's to give you some insight as to what I have in common with my current fiancée. Jillian was also married once before, and like me, she was widowed. Her husband, Michael, succumbed to cancer a few years before I lost my Samantha, and like me, she was simply trying to piece her life back together.

Then, the Fates decided to bring us together. I inherited my winery from a distant relative on my late wife's side of the family, which precipitated my move to Oregon. Jillian and I met, while I was investigating who would want to frame me for murder, and the rest, as they say, is history.

She and I hit it off so well that it startled the both of us. I, for one, couldn't believe that lightning could strike the same person twice. But, I'm happy to say, we enjoy each other's company, share many common interests, and have fallen head over heels for the other.

Like I said, life is good.

Returning back to the present day, here we were, walking hand-in-hand, through what had to be our favorite festival of the year. To be fair, our little town didn't have that many festivals, but this particular one was a doozy. It lasted at least three months long and involved just about every farm in the surrounding area, which included PV, Grants Pass, and Medford.

Farm fresh produce was available at roadside stands, which seemed to be around every bend in the road. The larger farms had dedicated barns and warehouses converted to storefronts. A few of the really big farms enjoyed the festivities so much that they not only opened up their shops, but rented out barn space and parts of their land. Why? Well, local merchants would set up shop and sell whatever they made: cutting boards, hand-crafted decorations, quilts, and so on. If you were looking for something, then you'd better believe someone here was trying to sell it to you.

Each progressive year, Cider Fest seemed to grow bigger. Around five years ago, I'm told, one of the farms decided to incorporate a corn maze into their available attractions. And yes, if you're familiar with my history, it's the very same one that Vance and I became hopelessly lost in, although we both maintain we had simply lost our bearings. Vance insisted he couldn't get lost. I insisted I could get lost anywhere, at any time. Care to guess who won that particular argument? Vance's only response was that some of my crappy sense of direction had to have rubbed off on him.

"Mom and Dad aren't going to make it back in time for Thanksgiving," Jillian was telling me, as we stopped at a small bakery stand selling fresh apple turnovers. They smelled so appetizing that I bought two of them. "I suggested we could get together once they're back, or else wait to celebrate at Christmas."

"How's Josh doing?" I asked.

Joshua Stanton Cooper just so happens to be Jillian's one and only sibling. I still haven't been able to meet the guy, seeing how he's currently an active duty Marine. The last time the poor guy had any time to himself was a few months before I became a resident of Oregon state, which we already know was a few years ago. Needless to say, our schedules *still* haven't been able to sync up.

"He always sounds so tired. This time, he was given two days. Only two days, Zachary. That poor man needs a solid two weeks of rest and relaxation."

"Didn't you tell me that he's currently on his fourth tour?"

"Yes. I know what you're thinking. He brings

this on himself. I'm just worried about him."

"Well, you're a good sister. I take it your parents are spending the day with him?"

"They were already in Virginia," Jillian told me, as she took a bite of her pastry. "This is good! Don't you think so? Anyway, Manassas isn't too far from Joshua's house, and he has RV parking on the side, so they'll spend the day there."

"Are you okay with that?" I asked.

One thing I knew about my fiancée was how close she was with her family. Holidays were all about coming together and spending time with one another. It had to be hard on her, since the only living members of her family were now on the opposite side of the country.

"I would have liked to have seen them," Jillian admitted, as she finished off her turnover, "but I understand their decision to stay put. After all, that's a long drive back home, and I would rather have my parents take their time driving such a long way."

"Understood."

"We were invited, you know."

"I know. If you'd like to join them, then you're more than welcome to go. I just wish I could go with you. I just don't feel right leaving the winery unprotected."

"Do you still think Abigail's family is going to try some type of retaliation?"

I sighed and nodded. "I wish I didn't, but I do. If ever there was a group who flat-out hated me, it'd be *that* one. No offense to my late wife, but that side of the family tree is just ... well, it's ..."

" ...bat-crap crazy?" Jillian slyly suggested. "No excuses needed. You're just trying to protect what you've created, and that particular family seems bent on trying to take it from you."

"They unarguably have it out for me. You know the history we have. I can only imagine what names I'm being called by the rest of the members of that whackjob bunch."

"As I told you before," Jillian told me, as she took my hands in hers, "if you are staying put, then I am staying put. We can just have our own get-together."

"Just the two of us?" I asked, perking up.

"Absolutely. Well ..."

"What's the matter?" I asked, after Jillian had trailed off.

"I just realized something. I don't think we're going to be the only ones who are spending Thanksgiving without our families."

"Oh? Is there someone else you're thinking of inviting?"

"There's Hannah and Colin, for a start. Provided she hasn't already made plans."

Hannah Bloom owned and operated the local florist shop in town, The Apple Blossom. She is newly single and, thanks to the ex-husband's messy divorce proceedings, not ready to mingle, if you catch my drift. She and her son, Colin, a bright, well-behaved boy of twelve, usually spend most waking hours in her shop. That is, unless Colin was in school.

Colin, I might add, was a big fan of the dogs, and had puppy sat for me a few times. I had no problem whatsoever in inviting those two over to our place for the holidays. One look at my face had Jillian beaming her million-dollar smile at me and reaching for her phone.

"Well, dinner for four it is," I announced. "That shouldn't be too bad."

"I'll see if she is going to be home this Thanksgiving," my fiancée said, as she pulled out her phone.

Busy tapping out a message on her smartphone, Jillian paused and looked up at me. Just like that, her smile was back as I saw her repeatedly tap her screen, as though she was now deleting her message. I groaned, flashed her my own smile, and then leaned back on the closest counter I could find.

"I know that smile. You've thought of someone else who might be left alone on Turkey Day. All right. Hit me with your best. Who else are you thinking about inviting? Oh, wait. I can probably guess this one. Taylor?"

Taylor Adams, owner of Farmhouse Bakery, also lived alone. She, like Hannah, was also divorced. Unlike Hannah, she didn't have any kids. She had admitted to Jillian, who had told me later, that she and her ex, Scott, married way too young, and Scott was more interested in making friends.

Female friends. In less than two weeks after Taylor and Scott had been married, he had been caught cheating on her.

Now, thanks to getting severely burned, Taylor had no desire to seek any romantic entanglement, either. I can say that I've spent time with Taylor, too, only I didn't know her as well as I did Hannah. Taylor is hard-working, dedicated, and therefore, put in some mighty long hours at her bakery.

Jillian nodded. "Yes. She only has Bentley to keep her company, and if you ask me, that isn't healthy."

Bentley, in case you're wondering, is a large, fluffy, black and grey tabby cat. Having met this cat a few times, I can tell you that he is one of the friendliest cats I have ever encountered. His purr, I kid you not, sounds like an idling diesel engine. Including his fur, he was almost as big as the corgis.

"Okey dokey. It could now be a party of five. That still isn't too bad."

"Umm, maybe plan for a party of eight?"

"Eight?" I repeated, as I turned to her. "Did I hear you right? Who else do you have in mind?"

"Well, we can't leave out Dottie."

Darla 'Dottie' Hanson was the only daughter of the recently deceased bookshop owner Clara Hanson. She was fairly new in town and was still getting used to owning and operating a business. Jillian has received her fair share of panicked phone calls from our new friend over the last two months, asking about inventory, how to properly receive a shipment of books, and so on. Dottie didn't have any family, either, and what's more, I knew that. I should have been the one to invite her over, seeing how I'm pretty sure she looked to the two of us as though we were her foster parents.

I shrugged. "I figured she was a given. And, I'm sorry to say, I kinda forgot about her. Just don't tell her that."

"It's a deal, Zachary."

"And that brings the count potentially to six. You said eight. Who else do you have in mind?"

"Lisa, and her girlfriend, Kimmi."

Ah, Lisa. I had forgotten about her, too. For those who don't know, Lisa Martinez is the person Jillian hired to run her bed and breakfast establishment, Highland House. In fact, I'm pretty sure Jillian *bought* that historic house with the sole intention of giving her friend a job. Maybe Lisa had mentioned, in passing, that she always wanted to run a bed and breakfast? Whatever. As for Kimmi, well, she was a reserved, quiet woman in her mid-twenties, who moved to PV from her home state of Hawaii late last year to be with her significant other. Truth be told, I do not know what type of work Kimmi does, seeing how I don't know much about her. As for Lisa, she was born and raised here, which explained how Jillian knew her. Kimmi, however, hails from Honolulu, and prior to their arrival, had never stepped foot in Oregon before.

Lisa is 29, Hispanic, and the world's biggest dog

lover. You think you love dogs? Think I do? We have nothing on this woman. She will actually get down on the ground and roll around with Sherlock and Watson, who then do their damnedest to climb her, as though they were goats, and as if she was a mound of rocks. Kimmi likes dogs, too, but will typically keep her emotions in check.

"All right. Let me get this straight. There could be you, me, Hannah, Colin, Taylor, Dottie, Lisa, and Kimmi? Did I miss anyone?"

"No, that's it. I have no idea if all of them will show up, but there's always that chance. You did say you were okay with this, didn't you?"

"Sure, I don't have a problem with it. Hmm, we're gonna need a big bird."

"I think you'd be surprised, Zachary. It's a common mistake, getting a bird that's simply too big. Oooo, this is going to be so much fun! We have so much to do before Thanksgiving arrives. We need to go shopping!"

One hour later, after dropping the dogs off at home, we stopped by the grocery store. One look at the practically full parking lot had me groaning. Apparently, everyone else in the town was preparing for the big day, too, even though it was still more than ten days out. But, I could only assume it would get worse before it would get any better. So, it was time to suck it up.

Stepping inside the store, both Jillian and I gasped with surprise. It was one panicked shopper away from an all-out stampede. As I had surmised, the place was already packed with people pushing fully laden carts every which way. Everyone seemed anxious to get to the other side of the store, regardless of where they were presently standing. Each person I saw had a look of grim determination on their face, as if they knew the success of their family's get-together depended on their ability to find a simple bag of mini-marshmallows. Stuffing mix, vegetables (canned, fresh, and frozen), whipped cream, eggs, flour, and the like, were piled so high that I briefly wondered if there was a limit to how much the carts could carry.

"Gary's Grocery sure is busy, isn't it?" Jillian observed. She pointed at a row of empty carts. "Would you?"

"You bet. Where do you want to start?"

"I always start at produce and work my way across. Zachary? Would you answer something for me? Truthfully, that is."

"Of course. What is it?"

"Do you like Thanksgiving as much as I do?"

"Please," I scoffed. "That has to be one of my favorite holidays of the year."

"Why?" Jillian wanted to know, as we stepped up to a large display of ears of corn. "What makes it your favorite?"

"The food, obviously. Think about it. Calories don't count on Turkey Day, so you can splurge as much as ..."

"Oh, yes they do," Jillian argued.

I waggled a finger and tried to look stern. "Oh, no they don't. Don't ruin it for me, lady. Repeat after me. Calories don't count on Thanksgiving."

Jillian giggled. "Very well. Calories don't count on Thanksgiving."

"What about you? What are your favorite parts of Thanksgiving?"

"Carrying out old traditions and starting new ones," Jillian said, with a sigh.

"You answered that awfully fast," I observed.

"It was an easy question. I love old family traditions. Speaking of which, does your family have any favorite recipes?"

"By that, I take it you'd like to know if I have any favorite recipes I look forward to each Thanksgiving?"

My fiancée's smile could have illuminated a darkened auditorium.

"Yes, exactly! What are some of your favorites? I'd like to make a few for you."

"Well, that's awful sweet of you. Let me think. Ooo, I know. Apple-cranberry crisp. My grandmother made it every year we got together. It was a thing, I guess. I loved it. Scarfed down every morsel I could get my hands on. Remember the crack about calories not counting? That's where it started."

"Do you have the recipe?" Jillian asked.

I shook my head. "No. I mean, *I* don't. But, I'm pretty sure my mom does."

"Good to know. Anything else?"

"Let's see. Samantha had a recipe for some seriously killer pumpkin bars with cream cheese frosting."

"That one has my vote," Jillian decided, as she selected some sweet potatoes and placed them in a bag. "I'll tell you now, if you can get that recipe to me, I'll make them for you."

"Deal! I should warn you, though. My family has been known to break out in bare-knuckle boxing to see who gets to take those leftovers home."

Jillian let out a delighted laugh. "They did no such thing."

"You're right. I'm pretty sure they settled it in a wrestling match. Hey, are you seriously going to make sweet potatoes?"

"It's a Thanksgiving tradition in my family," Jillian informed me. "I always have them. Why? Do you like sweet potatoes?"

"Umm, not really."

"Oh, that's too bad. They have really good flavor and the topping? I have a recipe that ... Zachary? What is that face for?"

"Sorry. I'm just not a fan."

"Mm-hmm. If I were to ask you how long it's been since you last tried sweet potatoes, what would your answer be?"

Uh, oh. I'm really going to have to work on keeping my emotions in check when conversing with my future wife. Somehow, and I wasn't sure how, she was able to look right through me and determine whether or not my objections to certain things were founded in fact or were pure BS.

"Umm, it might have been a while."

"What is a 'while'?" Jillian wanted to know.

"Umm ..."

Jillian turned to face me and put her hands on her hips. "Well? Be honest, Zachary."

"Fine. It might've been, say, oh, uh, 35 years or so ago."

"Zachary Michael! You cannot base your likes and dislikes from a simple taste test that happened decades ago! You were only a child back then. Do your siblings like them?"

I know I don't mention them too often, but I do have a younger brother and a younger sister. They're both still living in the Phoenix area, back in Arizona. Barry, who is five years younger than me, has three kids, and lives in Gilbert. He pretty much keeps to himself most of the time. Again, if I am to be honest with myself, I haven't really spoken with him much since Samantha passed. There's an uncomfortable silence between the two of us that neither of us know how to breach. My sister, Kira, lives in northern Phoenix and has a little boy. My mom tells me she's trying to adopt, seeing how she wants her son to have a brother. Whether or not that will happen, time will tell.

"Barry can't stand them, but I'm pretty sure Kira does. She never did have good taste, if you ask me."

Jillian harrumphed. "No one asked, Zachary. I'm making my mother's world-famous brown sugar pecan-topped sweet potatoes. It's always a hit."

"Hmm."

"You'll try some for me, won't you?"

"Umm..."

"Thank you, Zachary."

"Hey, wait a minute! I never agreed to try those things!"

"But you will. Thank you."

How was it possible to lose an argument without really having the argument in the first place?

"Well, if you're gonna make me try that, then I have something I'd like you to try."

Intrigued, Jillian hesitated at a stand displaying golden potatoes. "I'm listening."

"Sausage and apple dressing."

"You're talking about stuffing?"

"No, this doesn't go inside the bird, but is baked in a separate dish in the oven, instead."

Her eyes shot open. "You know the difference between stuffing and dressing? Zachary, I'm so impressed!"

"Samantha explained the difference to me years ago. For whatever reason, it stuck with me."

"Get me the recipe, and I'll make you a batch."

"Deal. I tell you, Thanksgiving cannot get here fast enough. To be able to smell ... what's the matter? You're frowning."

Jillian pointed at a large, empty cardboard tray, situated between the bagged carrots and bundles of herbs.

"They're out of cranberries. That can't be right. They're *never* out of cranberries."

"They probably just need to be restocked. I'll see if I can find someone."

"Thank you, Zachary."

It took only a few minutes to find a young produce clerk. Even though I could tell, with a single glance, he looked fairly harassed, as if he was having one of the worst days of his life, I had to ask.

"You're out of cranberries," I told the clerk. "I'm hoping you have some more in the back room?"

The clerk shrugged and helplessly shook his head. "I'm afraid not, sir. What we had, we put out. I can tell you it didn't last long."

"Oh. Do you know when you'll get some more in?"

"We're expecting a shipment in a few more days. I think I heard Gary say that he was going to try and push up the schedule, considering how busy we've been, but whether or not that happens, I don't know."

"All right. Thanks, kid."

"Any luck?" Jillian asked, moments later.

"They're out. He says their next shipment isn't due to arrive for a few more days."

"Well, I guess we have a little more time. I don't like waiting until the last minute to get the supplies I need."

I shrugged. "Maybe I should suggest to Caden that we should grow some cranberries at the winery?"

Caden Burne was the one-man show responsible for keeping my private winery, Lentari Cellars, running like a charm. He crafted the recipes, he oversaw the complex machinery, and he fielded all the decisions about when to plant, harvest, and so on. Essentially, he does it all. As for me? I'm the head of finance, which means all I'm responsible for is writing checks.

Jillian shook her head. "While it would be so very nice to have fresh cranberries, especially at this time of year, you'd be hard-pressed to grow them at your winery."

"Oh? How bad could it be? They're grown on bushes, aren't they? We have all kinds of berry bushes at the winery and have plenty of room. What's one more?"

"Oregon is one of the five states which produces cranberries," Jillian said, as she directed me to push our cart toward the first aisle of canned goods. "As for the cranberries themselves? They're grown on neither bush nor tree."

"Alrighty, Ms. Botanist Extraordinaire. What are they grown on?"

Jillian swatted my arm. "Plants. Low-growing plants, and if you ever see an actual cranberry plant in person, you'll see that they grow horizontal stems, or runners, which can get up to six feet in length."

"Damn," I whistled. "Still, we have plenty of room, so we could ..."

JEFFREY POOLE

"The problem comes from the harvest," Jillian interrupted. A few jars of various flavors of bouillon made their way into our cart, followed by several cartons of chicken stock. "You've seen how they do it, haven't you? Farmers typically flood the fields. The berries have four air pockets in them, so they'll float to the surface when they're picked."

"The harvest," I moaned. "I forgot about the 'wet method' of harvesting. Very well. Scratch that idea. I'm not flooding the winery. Hey, here's a thought. Could you use canned cranberries?"

"I'm going to buy a few, just to be certain we have some," Jillian told me, as we proceeded to the next aisle, which the hanging overhead sign identified as having Canned Fruit. "If we can get some … Zachary! They're out of canned cranberry sauce, too! This is getting frustrating."

That's just great. I could see what was brewing in my immediate future: a road trip to find some cranberries. As much as I didn't want to have to traipse all over town to track down a bag of those tart-as-hell red berries, I also didn't want Jillian to fret.

Swell.

Coming to the end of this particular aisle, we approached a large, open-air freezer which was stuffed to the brim with frozen turkeys. Now, let's see. Believe it or not, I actually knew the formula you're supposed to use in order to figure out what size of a bird you're going to need. Last time I checked, you needed a half pound of bird for each guest. Well, we were going to have eight people around our table, so that meant ... wait. That couldn't be right. We needed a four pound turkey? They didn't even make 'em that small, did they?

All right, Einstein. Let's check that math again.

Eight people, at half a pound each, would get you ... four pounds. Clearly, I had something wrong. Maybe it was a pound of bird for each guest? That would bring the total weight up to eight pounds, and for eight people, that still sounded like it'd be way too small.

So, where the hell was I screwing up?

"Penny for your thoughts?" Jillian sweetly asked me. "You seemed to be concentrating pretty heavily there. Is there anything I can do to help?"

"What size of bird are we going to need?" I asked, as I pointed at the frozen turkeysicles. "Isn't it half a pound of turkey for each person?"

Jillian shook her head. "Well, don't you like leftovers?"

"I *love* leftovers," I confirmed. "Turkey and cranberry sauce sandwiches? At all hours of the day? Hoo, boy. I think I just gained five pounds thinking about it."

"No cranberry sauce," Jillian reminded me.

"Yet," I softly murmured.

"I usually will go for a pound-and-a-half for each person. So, if we have eight people, then we should be looking for a twelve-pound bird."

I checked the tags. The weights of these birds

seemingly started at 16 pounds, and went up from there.

"These are some big birds. This one is 16.25. This one is 17.5. Holy moly, this one is over 20. You don't want one that big, do you?"

"To cook something that large, for as long as it needs, usually results in a dry turkey. I'd like to keep it as close to 12 as possible."

Some rapid rearrangement of turkeys in the freezer resulted in me finding a 14.9 pound bird.

"Close enough," Jillian decided. "If you would do the honors, kind sir."

"But of course, m'lady," I drawled, as I lifted the frozen turkey into the cart.

Just then, my cell began to ring, and based on the ringtone, which was *You Can Fly*, from Peter Pan (check my adventure with that blasted Egyptian mummy from a few years ago for an explanation), I knew it was Vance.

"Hey, Vance. What's up?"

"Hi, Zack. Are you busy?"

"I'm just helping Jillian at the grocery store. It's a mad-house in here. Seriously, Turkey Day is still …"

"Zack! Sorry to interrupt you, buddy, but I need you."

Detecting the seriousness of my friend's tone, I sobered. Jillian, catching the rapid change of expressions on my face, pulled the cart to the side to allow other shoppers around us.

"You have my attention. What's going on?"

"Care to go on a road trip?"

"What? To where?"

"Grants Pass."

As I mentioned earlier, Grants Pass is about 45 minutes away, due west. What could have happened where Vance would want a chaperone?

"Finish your shopping, go home, and grab the dogs. We're needed in Grants Pass."

"Is this for a case?" I asked. "Don't they have their own police force?"

"They do, but they're short-staffed. We're helping them out. Hurry, would you? A small grocery store over there has been vandalized. Their pharmacy was hit, but there's something about this case which doesn't sit right with me."

TWO

The distance from PV to Grants Pass could be covered in half an hour, provided you opened up the throttle once you were out on the freeway. And, don't get me wrong, there was a time when I would have done just that. However, those reckless, carefree days were long behind me, especially when I had my two dogs with me.

Obeying the rules of the road might be considered lame, and you were going to open yourself up to some serious ridiculing by your friends, but it was something I was unwilling to compromise. So, long story short, the dogs and I arrived in Grants Pass in just under an hour. The entire time I was driving, I kept asking myself, why this store? I've already passed nearly half a dozen different stores which could pass for grocery stores. Plus, I even passed a full-sized Safeway, something even PV doesn't have. So, what was so special about this one?

Spotting Vance's Oldsmobile sedan parked near the front of Vicki's Grab & Go, I took the empty spot next to his and, making sure the leashes were wrapped tightly around my hand, we approached the front entrance. However, I could see a long strip of yellow crime scene tape stretched across the glass double-doors. A uniformed officer stepped up to intercept us, but before he could say anything, the glass doors whooshed open and Vance stuck out his head.

"Zack! There you are. I was starting to worry you got lost, pal."

I waggled my cell phone. "Not likely. My phone walked me through all the way here. It gave perfect directions."

"Nice. You should be doing that all the time. Your sense of direction is so lousy that I'm sure you've probably misplaced your house a few times."

"Oh, hardy har har. I have not."

Well, okay, it might've happened once or twice, but I was never going to admit that to my police detective friend. Thankfully, I'm getting better with directions in the greater PV area, which might have something to do with me mastering the navigation system on my phone. I haven't been lost in a long while, which was a record for me, and I certainly didn't want to jinx myself now. When Vance wasn't looking, I quickly knocked on the side of my head, which had Sherlock head-tilting me.

"Welcome to Vicki's Grab & Go," my friend announced, as we all stepped into the store. "We need to ..."

"Wait," I interrupted. I then pointed at a display rack of fresh French bread. "This is a grocery store. There's food in there. I don't think we're supposed to be here. I mean, *they* aren't."

Vance turned to point at an older, middle-aged brunette, who was chatting with several police officers.

"That's Vicki. She's the owner of this place. She's already given me permission to... scratch that. Hey, Vicki? Er, Ms. Doyle? Could I borrow you for just a moment?"

The woman in question turned at the sound of her name and smiled at Vance. Just then, Sherlock decided to give himself a good shaking, and I watched a frown immediately appear on Ms. Doyle's face. Then again, I also watched her drop her gaze to the ground and, after locating the source of the jingling collar, instead of ordering us out of her store, her eyes lit up. She hurried over to us.

"Ooo, tell me this is the famous Sherlock and Watson I've heard so much about!"

I pointed each of them out. "This is Sherlock. He's the one with black on his coat. Watson is over there, with the red and white fur. Sounds like you already know my dogs, huh?"

Even though Ms. Doyle was wearing a very tight, knee-length skirt, she managed to squat down next to the dogs to give each of them a friendly scratching behind the ears. Both corgis, I might add, immediately rolled onto their backs. I swear, neither of them had a shred of dignity between them.

"Are you going to help me find out who did this? I'll bet you could figure this out with your eyes closed, couldn't you, my handsome little boys?"

"Uh, Watson is a girl," I quietly corrected.

"Oh, you are? What kind of name is that for such a pretty little girl like you?" Vicki all but cooed.

I noticed the smirk forming on Vance's face, who had long maintained that I had picked a lousy name for my female corgi. Scowling, I cocked my arm back, as if I was ready to throw a punch. And, let's face it. I was.

Vance took a few steps away from me. "Ms. Doyle, may I present Zack Anderson, and his two dogs, Sherlock and Watson. They are official police consultants, and they are ..."

"I know why they're here," Vicki smoothly interrupted. "Mr. Anderson? I don't normally allow animals in my store, but you and your dogs have my full blessing to check wherever you'd like. Find the bastards who did this."

"We'll do our best," I promised.

Vance tapped me on the shoulder and pointed at the opposite end of the store, where the tiny pharmacy was situated. We could see a metal gate had been lowered, to securely prevent anyone from gaining access after hours. However, we could both see that the gate had been ripped from the wall, as though someone had hooked a chain to the gate and then sped off. In a semi.

I whistled as we examined the destruction. "Someone really wanted in there, didn't they?"

Vance leaned over the counter to see for himself what had happened to the pharmacy. What he saw had him cringing. Me, too, for that matter.

Racks were destroyed. Shelves were broken. Several cabinet doors were open. One was even hanging off of its one good hinge. But the most alarming thing we discovered? A severe lack of pills. Practically all the pill bottles had been taken. I couldn't even begin to fathom what that might have been worth. Sure, the pharmacy was small, as pharmacies go, but come on. You know as well I do how much those pills are generally worth.

"I'm hoping everything is insured," I quietly murmured.

Vance eyed me with an unreadable expression. "Right? Okay, let's get to work. Why don't you walk the dogs around and see if they can pick up anything."

"You got it."

Gathering up the leashes, I walked around the small area behind the pharmacy counter, but neither dog, I could tell, was interested in the slightest. Sherlock sniffed once at a discarded pill bottle, but that was the *only* reaction I could get out of them. Growing frustrated, I decided to walk around the perimeter of the store and see if there might be something, *anything*, that was worth investigating.

We started on the eastern side of the store, which was where you'd find produce. Now, I realize I have never worked in the produce department at a grocery store, and therefore didn't really know what I was looking for, but everything appeared normal to me. Displays of avocados, tomatoes, and bananas were stacked neatly on tables. Oranges and kiwis shared a corner display, and several varieties of apples were layered in makeshift pyramids here and there.

Catching sight of a swinging double door just to my left, I poked my head in to see what must be the area where the produce clerk would unbox the fruit and veggies and dispose of the packaging. Both Sherlock and Watson jammed their heads through the flap, too, and studied the scene before them, and then—disinterested—moved on.

We swung around the back of the store, where the deli and butcher block were located. The dogs only stopped at the deli after detecting I had stopped first. Whatever they were cooking smelled fantastic. Roast chicken, maybe? Barbecue sausage? Whatever it was, it had the effect of reminding me it was close to dinnertime.

We hit the dairy, walked up and down the fourteen aisles that comprised the store, but all without a hit. That is, until we hit the far back corner, which revealed another set of double doors, this time leading to the grocery store's back store-room. I took a quick look back there, too, only I didn't see anything out of the ordinary. Sherlock wanted to look, and after allowing him and Watson a few moments to peruse the scene, I pulled them back out and headed toward the front of the store.

Sherlock, the little booger, resisted.

"Stop stopping, Sherlock. There's nothing to see back there. We're going this way, okay? Now, stop resisting and …"

Just like that, the two corgis dropped their objections and, suddenly, I was the one being pulled along. Curious as to where we were going, I tried to see around the dogs, but didn't have much luck, since they were first pulling to the left, then to the right, and finally, back to the left.

"Are you looking for the door?" I finally asked. I pointed out the one we had come in. "Look, there's one over there. Now, would you please pick a direction? Left or right, I don't care."

Watson chose right. Sherlock chose left. My arms were yanked in both directions, effectively turning me into a human-shaped T.

"Ouch," I complained to the dogs. "Thanks for that. You want to go outside? Fine. Watson, come with me. We're going to follow Sherlock."

Once outside, both corgis shook themselves, looked up at the bright, blue sky, and headed off. At least it was in the same direction this time.

"Are you guys heading somewhere?" I heard

Vance inquire.

He clearly had followed us outside and was now slowly walking behind us.

"Beats me. I have no idea where they're planning on going. They may not have found anything inside, but it looks like we're on the trail of something out here."

I watched Vance have an internal argument with himself as he debated whether or not he should follow us. Looking at the two corgis staring up at him, expectantly, turned the tide in their favor.

"Fine. Let's go."

I gave the dogs some slack in their leashes and decided to see where they'd lead us. The dogs promptly took us over to the sidewalk and, as though they were out for a walk in the park, strutted along the street like AKC champions who had just won Best in Show. We watched quite a few people slow their cars and watch the dogs go by. Not one of them, I'd like to add, bothered to look our way, namely myself and Vance.

"They love the attention, don't they?" Vance quietly observed.

"That they do. Where are we headed? What's down this way?"

"More storefronts," Vance said, as he looked off in the distance. "We're just about to hit downtown. Goes to show you how small this town really is."

"PV is way smaller," I argued.

"True. Maybe they caught the scent of the burglar and are following him to his hideout? Maybe Vicki has a few enemies who might … Zack? Where are they going now?"

Sherlock and Watson had veered the moment the road forked. It looked as though we were headed for an alley that ran between two of the busiest streets in downtown Grants Pass. Skeptical, I glanced at my dogs, who were pulling at their leashes, anxiously awaiting permission to resume walking. Shrugging, I gave them slack and followed them into the alley.

Barely wide enough to fit a garbage truck, this alley was one-way, had small green dumpsters on either side for each of the merchants, and didn't smell that great. Then again, what would you expect if you had that many dumpsters in such close proximity? Exasperated, I looked over at Vance, who was moments away from pulling up his shirt to cover his nose.

"Well, that's an attractive smell," my detective friend decided. "Sherlock? Watson? What's in here you want us to see? Or smell? The sooner we find what you want, the sooner we can get out of here."

"Agreed. Come on, guys. What do you…"

I trailed off as Sherlock suddenly angled for the closest dumpster and then sniffed along the bottom of it once we neared. The little corgi turned to look up at me, glanced once at the dirty, crud-covered asphalt, and whined. Thankful he wasn't trying to sit, which is what he usually did when he found something worth checking out, I handed the leashes to Vance and hurried over to the dumpster.

"Be careful," Vance warned. "We don't know what's in there. For all we know, it could be some high-as-a-kite junkie."

I carefully lifted the lid and peered inside. Surprised, I pushed the lid off the dumpster, allowing it to smack noisily against the cinderblock wall behind it. I held a hand out to Vance.

"Gloves."

Vance reached inside his jacket and pulled out a pair of latex gloves. Snapping them on, I gingerly started to reach inside when I thought better of it. Cursing to myself, I pulled out my phone and clumsily activated the camera app. Holding it up and over the rim of the dumpster, I took a few photos.

"Whatcha got?" Vance asked. "What's in there?"

Putting my phone away, I reached inside the dumpster and pulled out a dark green duffel bag. This *had* to be what the dogs wanted. After all, there was nothing else in the dumpster but bags of garbage.

"What do you have there?" Vance wanted to know.

I let the duffel bag plop to the ground, but not before each of us noticed the telltale rattle from what sounded like hundreds of small objects striking one another. Like ... pills?

"No way," Vance breathed. He snapped on his own pair of gloves and hurriedly unzipped the bag. Sure enough, it was filled to the brim with various bottles of pills. They *had* to be the ones stolen from Vicki's pharmacy. But, why dispose of them here? I mean, didn't these things have some type of street value to them?

It didn't make any sense.

"I told you something was off here," Vance muttered.

He zipped the bag up and pointed back the way we had come.

"Let's get out of here. I need some fresh air."

"What do you think it means?" I asked my friend, as we returned to Vicki's store. "Why go through all the trouble of stealing the pills in the first place, only to throw them away in some dumpster nearly half a mile away? Does that make sense to you?"

Vance shook his head. "No, it doesn't."

"You said something felt 'off' about this whole mess. Care to share?"

"I don't know, buddy," Vance said, as we approached the bustling activity in front of the store. "There's something we're missing here. Check it out. The smashed glass of the front window here? See for yourself. There's more chunks of broken glass on the *outside* of the store than the *inside*. What does that tell you?"

"That whoever broke it did so from the inside the store," I decided. "But, that doesn't make any sense either, does it? I mean, you're trying to get in, not out."

"It makes sense if you're trying to cover something up," Vance argued. "If I didn't know any better, then I'd say the hit on the pharmacy was to draw our attention away, but away from *what*? That's what I want to know."

The store owner came hurrying out the front door of her store.

"There you are. Detective Samuelson, what is the meaning of wandering away for a leisurely walk? Why aren't you looking for this burglar? I was told your police department had a high success rate of closed cases, yet I haven't seen anything that could closely resemble a ... what's that?"

Vance pulled the duffel bag from his shoulder, unzipped it, and nonchalantly tossed it onto the ground. The bag immediately split open, revealing hundreds of bottles inside.

"Those are the pills that were stolen from your store. We found them in a dumpster nearly half a mile away. You're welcome."

The three police officers representing the GPPD gawked at the bag before turning to look back at us. As one, all three officers then dropped their gaze to Sherlock and Watson, who were panting contentedly on the sidewalk. Sherlock's jaws opened and his long tongue flopped out.

"How in the world ..." one officer began.

"Don't ask," I interrupted, giving the friendly

officer a smile. "I've yet to figure out how they do it."

"Man, we need to petition the captain for our own K-9 unit," I heard one officer say, as we walked away.

I felt the leashes go taut and automatically looked down. Both dogs were back on their feet and both, I might add, were straining to pull me through the front door of the grocery store. Was there something in there they wanted me to see?

"Now what?" Vance asked, from somewhere behind me.

"Who the hell knows?" I grumbled. "You'd think I'd be familiar enough with these types of practices to not be surprised, but noooo. Come on, guys. Show me what's gotten you riled up, okay?"

We carefully made our way back through the store. Sensing movement from behind me, I could see that not only was Vance following us, but so were the three GP cops, as well as several of their crime scene techs and Ms. Doyle herself. Noticing we were angling for the far corner of the store once more, I suddenly knew where we were headed.

"Why do I get a feeling I should have paid attention to you the first time?" I muttered.

"What's that?" Vance wanted to know.

I pointed at the doors leading to the back storeroom. "The dogs wanted to go in there before. We all poked our heads in, and when it became apparent that the burglar must've avoided that area, I ignored it. Sherlock, if memory serves, wasn't happy about it."

"Let's see where he wants to go this time around," Vance suggested.

"You got it. All right, Mr. Know-it-all. Let's see what you can find back here, okay?"

I heard Sherlock snort, as if to say, *challenge accepted.*

We pushed our way through the swinging doors and gathered just inside the stock room. I could see a small counter on the right, which had several shipping invoices lying about. I assumed (correctly) that this was where they handled all the store's deliveries. Further exploration revealed the presence of a machine that was present in quite a few grocery stores, seeing how the vast majority of deliveries into the store came in boxes.

It was a cardboard baler. Throw the boxes in *there*, press that button *there* and then keep your arms and fingers way the hell out of harm's way. In fact, there was a bale of cardboard, already smooshed and trussed up, sitting on a palette by one of two loading doors.

"Where do you want to go, guys?" I asked the dogs, as the crowd of people behind us continued to grow.

Sherlock sniffed along the ground, looked up briefly to study the baler, and then turned left. Glancing that way, I could see a large walk-in freezer, with a heavy winter coat hanging on a peg beside it. This time, both dogs sat by the freezer's door, as if they were waiting for me to open it and allow them in.

"Nuh-uh," I said, frowning. "That's not gonna happen, your Royal Canineships." I heard several snickers from behind me. "That's the freezer. Inside there, you'll find some seriously inhospitable conditions, and for a little dog like you, you wouldn't last very long. I'd rather not turn you two into corgi-sicles, so ... no. Not happening."

Watson whined.

I shook my head. "Not happening, Watson."

"Awwwwoooooowwooooowwwoooowooo."

Practically everyone behind me burst out laughing. Sherlock had let out one of his argumentative howls, as if he was telling *me* how things were going to play out. Squatting beside the feisty corgi, I draped an arm over his back and tousled his fur.

"Sherlock, it's cold in there. Really freakin' cold. You don't want to go in there."

Sherlock was adamant. He apparently believed the freezer needed to earn his corgi Stamp of Approval and wasn't prepared to let the matter drop. I sighed, glanced back at the group of people behind us, and then hooked a thumb at the door.

"Tell me I'm wrong. It's just a freezer, right?"

Vicki nodded. "That's right. What's the matter? Is Sherlock saying there's something wrong with my freezer?"

"Well, he's sitting, and he typically does that after a search, whenever he finds what he's searching for. He truly believes something is in there and it needs our attention."

Vicki turned and motioned to a tall, heavyset guy I hadn't noticed before.

"This is my assistant manager, Brian. He's been with me for several years now. Brian, would you do the honors?"

"What am I looking for, ma'am?"

Vicki looked back at me and gave me a questioning look. I ended up shrugging and looking down at the dogs, as though I expected them to field the question. After a few moments, I shrugged again.

"I really don't know how to answer that. You obviously have been in there before, right?"

Brian nodded. "Many times, sir."

"Perfect. You're just the one to do this. Since you've been in there so many times, then I would suggest you look for something out of the ordinary. Is there something there that doesn't belong? Maybe check the freezer itself? I'd check to make sure someone hasn't tampered with the controls, so that it would fail at a future date. Just make sure everything is working okay, I guess. That's where I'd start."

Vicki was nodding. "Yes, I like that. Do that, please."

Brian nodded. "Yes ma'am. If you'd all like to wait here, then I'll take care of this."

The assistant manager took the coat off the peg, slipped it on, and zipped it up. Looking like he should now be handling a team of sled dogs in the midst of a race through Alaska, Brian slipped inside the freezer. Within moments, we heard boxes being slid along the floor.

"Think he'll find anything in there?" I quietly asked.

"You know your dogs better than anyone," Vance replied. "If there's something there that needs to be seen, then something tells me our new pal Brian will be the one to find it."

"Do you have any idea what that could be?" the store owner asked us, as she looked over at Vance, and then me.

Vance shrugged. "You don't keep anything of value in there, do you?"

"In our freezer? Heavens no."

"You weren't storing anything in there that shouldn't be there, were you?" I asked, already knowing what the answer was going to be.

"Of course not. What are you suggesting?"

Vance scratched the side of his head. "Well, we may ..."

At that point, the freezer door opened and Brian hurried out. Sealing off the door, and pulling the jacket off, the assistant manager took Vicki by the arm and pulled her away. Once they were safely out of earshot, I could hear some type of hushed conversation between the two of them, but they were too far away to make it out.

"He *did* find something," I breathed, as I lowered my voice to a whisper. I squatted next to

Sherlock and motioned Watson over. "Good job, you two. What do you guys think? Some type of smuggling operation? Or, more likely, you've tracked down that elusive steak you think you two deserve?"

I heard someone snicker behind me.

Sherlock gave me such a look of derision that I suddenly became worried. Not for retaliation, mind you, but for what had been found. Keeping an eye on the hushed conversation happening between store owner and assistant manager, I strained my hearing in an attempt to hear what the two were talking about.

"Can you make anything out?" Vance wanted to know.

I shook my head no. "The only word I've caught is 'box.' Maybe Brian found an extra box or two in there?"

"Someone broke in here," Vance reminded me. "I doubt very much someone broke in to stash something in there. No, I'd put my money on something being stolen."

Vance was right. It turned out that not one, nor two, but three boxes were missing. Even though it's possible to misplace a box or two, especially in a freezer of that size, I was assured that Brian personally signed for the delivery last night. He had placed the three boxes in the freezer, along with the rest of the shipment, and promptly locked everything up for the night.

Now, however, the boxes were missing, and as

far as anyone could tell, no one had even known those boxes existed. But, Brian showed us where he had left the boxes (inside that frigid freezer), and now, that particular corner of the huge icebox was empty.

"What was in the boxes?" Vance wanted to know.

"Let's see. Those were boxes MDC2146, MDC2147, and MDC2148."

"MDC?" I curiously repeated. "Does that mean something?"

"Medford Distribution Center," Brian translated. "It's where we get all of our shipments. Those three boxes? Well, it stinks to have to admit this, especially at this time of the year, but those boxes contained something we were desperately needing. Ms. Doyle, I'm sorry to announce this, but those missing boxes will mean we will continue to be short of cranberries."

Vicki Doyle sighed and uttered a very unlady-like curse.

THREE

T here are pros and cons to everything you do in life. If something is deemed too good to be true, then rest assured, it probably is. For instance, if you're given a fantastic 'new' automobile, only it happens to be a 90-year-old classic, you can't possibly expect automotive machinery to run every time you twist the key.

I'm referring, of course, to my 1930 Ruxton sedan, given to me by my fiancée after she discovered the classic roadster had been included with the purchase of Highland House last year. This was the very same car driven by Dame Hilda Highland, and had sat in storage for nearly 70 years. Thankfully, Dame Highland had enlisted the services of a local gas station to keep the car in pristine condition, and arranged for its maintenance even after she was gone. That doesn't account for much when the current owner, yours truly, has, er, difficulty driving that mechanical beast.

Let me explain.

The art of driving a stick-shift vehicle is rapidly disappearing throughout this country. Most people prefer 'automatic' vehicles versus those with manual transmissions. If you want to be honest, I was the same way. However, I *did* learn how to drive on a Subaru with a manual transmission, with my grandmother in the passenger seat.

What an eye-opening experience that turned out to be. Fast forward to the present day, and even though I haven't driven a stick for what seems like eons, I have never forgotten how. At least, I thought I still knew.

Enter the Ruxton. This beauty was also a manual transmission, but instead of the standard six gears, which means first gear is in the top left position, and fifth gear is in top right, with reverse directly below that and … Let me show you what I mean. The referral diagram on the shifting knob looks like this:

For the Ruxton, however, it has only three gears, plus reverse. The problem was how it was laid out. First was *not* in the top left corner, but directly below that, in the bottom left corner, which was where I'm used to seeing second gear. Then, second and third gear were on the right, in their respective locations. The diagram for it, as many of you have already guessed, looks something like this:

H

So, every time I brought the car to a stop, and then tried to ease it forward, I ended up jamming it into reverse, and going the opposite direction. Right. That explains the small dents on the bumper. And first gear? Pssht. I keep shifting into second by mistake, since it was in the 'up' position which explains the need for a new starter (I kept stalling it out). Finally, seeing how I keep forgetting the locations for the correct gears, the Ruxton sounded as though it needed a new clutch assembly, and probably a new transmission. But, do you think there are that many mechanics who are willing to look at an example of automotive technology that's older than their grandparents?

That was why I was currently back at Rupert's Gas & Auto, trying to explain to Vince Rupert himself, why the car he and his predecessors had taken care of for decades now sounded like the Clampett's jalopy from that campy TV show with the catchy theme song.

"Holy crap, Zack. What in the Sam Hill did you do to the old gal? She was in cherry condition when we gave her back to you!"

"Umm ..."

"Having troubles driving it?"

"Well, the gears take some getting used to."

"The gears? You talkin' 'bout the transmission? It's a standard H. It's a piece of cake. Don't you know how to drive a stick?"

My face flamed up. "Yeah, I do, only it didn't drive like that. Look, I know I screwed it up. That's why I'm here. I'm hoping you can fix it back up for me."

"Just the transmission?"

"Umm …"

"You did something else to the poor girl, didn't you?" Vince accused. "Spill. What happened?"

"I, er, might've backed into a few things by mistake, seeing how Reverse is in the wrong freakin' spot."

Vince walked around the car to look at the bumper. He whistled.

"Is it bad?" I hesitantly asked.

"I've seen worse. I can get those hammered out for you."

"And …"

"There's more?" He sounded incredulous. "What else?"

"Umm, you might need to look at the starter. But, that's it. I swear."

"It'll probably take a couple of weeks," Vince told me, as he ran a hand through his slick-backed hair. "Finding parts is becoming difficult. The last time I worked on this transmission, I had to have several parts fabricated, since they weren't being made any more."

"Just do the best you can. You know I'm good for the repairs, pal."

"I know you are, Mr. Anderson. Me and my boys will take care of it. She'll be as good as new before you know it. Maybe then, I can show you the tricks I've learned in keeping the old girl happy."

I grinned and held out a hand. "Deal."

"Do you need a ride back anywhere?"

"Could you give me a lift to Jillian's place? Er, I mean, Cookbook Nook? That's where I left the dogs."

"You got it. Let me find Dean. He'll give you a lift wherever you need to go."

"Thanks. How's he doing?"

Young Mr. Dean Rupert got his hands royally slapped when he and his friend, who happened to be Captain Nelson's grandson, committed a theft a couple of years ago.

"Who, Dean? Surprisingly, he's keeping himself out of trouble." Vince chuckled as he took the Ruxton's keys and hung them on a peg behind the counter. "Then again, I'm sure it had something to do with an agreement he and I made."

"Which was?" I prompted.

"If he screws up in the slightest, and that includes *anything* he's doing, then his sorry butt will be joining the military."

Right on cue, a tall, lanky teenager appeared and caught the keys his father had tossed in his direction.

"Take Mr. Anderson to 3rd and Main. He's going to Ms. Cooper's place."

The kid nodded sullenly and, without bothering to see if I was following, headed for the door. Whether or not the kid recognized me, I couldn't say, as he didn't utter a single word to me for the entire drive. Offering him a thanks as I exited the small truck, I headed for Cookbook Nook, where I was greeted by two over-enthusiastic corgis.

"Hi, guys. Did you miss me?"

Sherlock crouched low, stretched, and licked my hand. Watson shoved her way past Sherlock and presented herself for her own fair share of scratches. I looked up as I noticed Jillian headed my way.

"So, is it going to survive?"

"It lives to fight another day," I announced. "I really thought I had the gears down, but clearly, I don't. Vince said that the transmission looked pretty well chewed up. And, as long as he was at it, he'll pop out the dents on the bumper."

"What did you hit, again?" Jillian asked.

"The, er, handicapped sign in front of Hidden Relic Antiques was the latest. Burt was laughing at me, for so long, that I had to pull over to make sure he wasn't going to have a heart attack."

"Did you apologize for hitting his sign?" Jillian asked, as she dabbed at the corners of her eyes with a tissue.

My brow furrowed as I noticed my lovely fiancée was enjoying herself at my expense. "I did, as a matter of fact. He said I didn't need to worry about it. Then, he did the damnedest thing. He walked over to the sign, placed a hand on it, and straightened it back up himself."

Jillian whistled. "Impressive."

"He was still laughing as he went back inside," I continued. "Then, just to satisfy my own curiosity, I tried to move that sign on my own. Flippin' thing didn't budge."

For the record, Burt Johnson was a former Army Ranger. He was in his early sixties, had spiky gray hair cut in a military-style fashion, and had to be at least six and a half feet tall. And ripped. Did I mention that? I still maintain I've seen the guy pushing a 747 *uphill* in those World Strongman contests. He denies it, of course.

"Do you still want to go? I told you before, you don't need to go with me. I know this type of thing really isn't your style."

I looked back at her and grinned. "Going to a florist doesn't really appeal, but going to one with you? I can get on board with that."

"Right answer, Mr. Anderson."

"Why thank you, Ms. Cooper."

"You two are too cute," one of Jillian's employees gushed.

Turning, I could see that it was Cassie, a young black-haired girl who has worked for Jillian for several years now. In fact, I think she might have just been made Assistant Manager. Both of us gave the girl a grin as she moved back behind the counter to help a customer.

Twenty minutes later, we were stepping out of Jillian's SUV and approaching Pomme Valley's biggest and best florist, The Apple Blossom. Yes, before you ask, it's the only florist shop in town.

Why not just come out and say it was the only one? Well, when it comes to describing the different businesses which called PV home, I find myself saying that a lot. So, I'm trying to break myself of the habit.

Commotion across the street drew my attention. I could see the Red Barn Tavern, and I immediately thought of my adventures with the misfit thrill-seeker club from a few months ago. I had joined up at the request of Vance, who was helping a visiting U.S. Marshal locate a missing fugitive. Wow, I won't be forgetting that anytime soon.

"Hey, Bacchus!"

Hand still on the door, about to follow Jillian inside, I turned. It was Yeti, who had taken over leadership of the club.

"Hey, Yeti," I returned, as I let the door close and turned to my (sad to admit) much younger friend. "What's new with you guys?"

"Have you changed your mind? We still have some openings on our zip-line excursion, happening at Cottonwood Canyon State Park next week."

My eyebrows shot up. I had already given Yeti my answer, and it matched Vance's: no.

"Yeah, not this time. Remove heights from the equation and you'll have a much better chance of getting me to go."

"Funny you should say that," Yeti said, grinning. "We're thinking about doing a deep-water dive just before Christmas. Some ship has been discovered in Monterey, and it's finally been cleared for exploration."

"The San Agustin?" I dryly asked.

"You know it? Right on, Bacchus! Are you with us? You mentioned you had your SCUBA certification, didn't you?"

"I did, and I do," I told my friend. "That would be a trip worth going on. Obviously, the aquarium has pulled everything they needed from it. I'm surprised they'll let people enter it."

"They won't," Yeti admitted. "We can observe, but don't touch and don't approach. It'll still be worth visiting."

"Let me talk it over with Vance, and we'll get back to you, okay?"

Pleased, Yeti slapped a friendly hand on my shoulder. "Glad to hear it, Bacchus. Keep me informed! I'll save a couple of spots for you!"

Thinking back to the fun times we had while vacationing in Monterey earlier this year, I opened the door and led the dogs inside. From the moment we stepped through the door, it felt — and smelled — as if we were in another world. The petrichor wafting up from the recently watered plants had me sighing contentedly. Both dogs immediately stopped, lifted their noses to sample the air a few times, and then looked up at me with hopeful eyes.

I knew that look. They were hoping I'd unhook the leashes and let them have free rein to explore the store. I can only imagine that, in their eyes, there must be a million different things to smell in here, which explained why both dogs were whining and pulling on their leashes.

I caught sight of Jillian inspecting a large purple flower arrangement on my left, and immediately headed that way. She smiled at me as she saw me approaching, and then disappeared from sight. Laughing, I decided to see where the corgis wanted to go, instead.

I was led over to a large helium tank and several filled mylar balloons. Glancing up, I could see 'Happy Birthday', 'Happy Anniversary', and 'Congrats' balloons, all in various colors. I felt a sharp tug on the leash. Looking down at Sherlock, I saw that he had positioned himself in such a way that he was looking up at the clutch of balloons, but from about five feet away, thus allowing him to see the flip-side of the clutch of balloons.

Guiding Watson over, the three of us studied the floating balloons. One balloon, a bright, neon green one which had a flower shape, had Happy 7th Birthday printed on it. Shrugging, I pulled the dogs away, only … you guessed it … the dogs didn't budge.

"What? It's just a balloon. It's not gonna hurt you guys, okay? Let it go."

Both dogs remained mired to the spot. Sighing, I pulled out my phone and snapped a picture of the balloon, with the intent to humor them. But, much to my surprise, as soon as I slid my phone back into my pocket, they were both up and moving around. In fact, they had just noticed Jillian appear from behind a cluster of long-stemmed white roses and quickly morphed into their Clydesdale personas to get me over to her as quickly as possible.

I briefly wondered what I would look like if I wasn't wearing shoes, but socks. Would it look like I was waterskiing on the tiled floor? Probably.

Jillian leaned up against the counter and looked for Hannah. We couldn't see her anywhere, but we could hear her. Her voice was already soft to begin with, but there was something about the way she was talking which made us think she was on the phone, and the call wasn't going as planned. Jillian pointed at the closed Staff Only door and held a finger to her lips.

"I won't talk about it here," Hannah's voice was saying. "No. You've heard my answer. I can't go anywhere right now. Mom, I've given my answer. I will not close up, not even for a day. I can't afford to. Please, don't ask me again, okay? Good. Thank you. Love you, too, Mom. We'll see you for Christmas, don't worry."

"I don't think we should've heard that," I whispered. I pointed at the far wall, where a refrigerated glass case displayed a variety of arrangements. "We'll be over there."

Jillian patted my hand. "Thank you, Zachary. I'll deal with this."

"Does she get the official invite?"

Jillian nodded, just as the small office door opened. Hannah's eyes widened appreciatively, and she smiled.

"Jillian! What a wonderful surprise! What can I do for you today?"

Leaving the two women to begin their hushed conversation, the dogs and I wandered over to inspect the arrangements. And, let me just say, holy moly. A flower arrangement, done professionally, can cost you upwards of $100. And the ones in this case? The lowest I found was $75, and they went all the way up to $169. I was starting to think that Hannah had her flowers waaayyy overpriced, but in the few minutes I was in front of the display case, no fewer than three guys had appeared, made their selections, and took them to the front counter. Not one of them looked at the price tag, by the way. I guess when you were in the dog house, the amount you were willing to pay to get back in your significant other's good graces ranked fairly low on the totem pole of priorities.

I heard one of the dogs shake their collar. Just like that, we were off again, only this time, we seemed to be headed toward a long work bench. I could see strands of discarded plants (baby's breath?), the clippings from (I'm guessing) long-stemmed roses, and scraps of various colors of polypropylene. Sitting off to the side of the counter, totally engrossed in some type of game on his tablet computer, was Colin, Hannah's son.

Colin is a fairly shy kid who doesn't make friends too easily. He has the slim build of his mother, and the looks (I'm told) of his father:

brown hair and blue eyes. I've talked to the kid a few times before, and have learned he's a bright boy who loves school, and is considered one of the smartest. That, however, hasn't made him too many friends, and as a result, he typically keeps to himself.

However, the one thing I've learned about the boy is that he absolutely loves dogs. He's the only one who can give Sherlock and Watson a run for their money in the high energy department. The last time we dropped the dogs off at Hannah's house and had the boy watch them for the night, the dogs were so exhausted after we picked them up that I had to ask Hannah if they had stayed up all night.

Sherlock yipped a greeting. Colin's head jerked up, and he leaned over the counter to see two sets of eyes staring up at him. The boy was all smiles.

"It's Sherlock and Watson! Hi, guys!"

Both dogs darted around the corner, each intent on making it to one of their known playmates before the other one could. Colin dropped to the ground and started giving them scratches.

"What are you two up to today, you hairy little squirts?"

Both dogs writhed on the floor in apparent ecstasy.

"You've got their number," I observed.

Colin looked up at me. I'm sorry to say that I actually witnessed the boy's cheery disposition withdraw into himself as he became the quiet, shy boy once more.

"Hello, Mr. Anderson."

I was determined to put him at ease.

"Hey there, sport. How's it goin'? Whatcha playin' there?"

Colin looked over at his tablet computer and shrugged. "It's a game called WordPiles." The tablet was pushed along the counter until it was in front of me. "Do you know how to play?"

Oddly enough, I did.

"Yeah, you have to find words in that jumble there. You can look here, above the letters, and see how many words are left to find. See this? There are four missing four-letter words, two five-letter words, and three seven-letter words. Need some help?"

"Only if you think you can find them," Colin told me. "If I can't find them, then I don't see how you can…"

The boy trailed off as I quickly found word after word. After about thirty seconds, I slid the completed puzzle back to him.

"Wow! How'd you do that?"

I spread my hands in a helpless gesture. "Hey, what can I say? I'm a writer. Plus, I grew up playing video games. Pac-Man, Dig Dug, and Donkey Kong, just to name a few."

"Wow," Colin softly muttered. "Old school. Those are my favorites, too."

It was my turn to be surprised. "Really? Since when? The graphics on the games nowadays are so much better than what we had when I was your age."

"Have you seen what games are popular right now?" Colin returned. "Shoot-em-ups. War games. Alien invasions. Zombies. Those aren't fun. Gives me anxiety just thinking about it."

I stared at the boy and had to chuckle. A smile formed on my face as I realized how I could reach this kid.

"So, you think you're good on old retro games, is that it? What's your favorite?"

"Probably one you wouldn't know," Colin said, sighing. He reached for his tablet. "You're trying to save the last human family from nasty robots. You use two joysticks, one to move the little man across the screen, and the other to fire his weapon."

I nodded and pretended to think. "Do the graphics remind you of Defender?"

Colin's eyes lit up. "Yeah, they do! How do you know? Have you played it before?"

"I'm pretty sure I have. I think you're talking about one of my all-time favorite games."

"No way," Colin decided. "You're telling me you've played Robotron? But ... you're old!"

"There's no such game," I told the young boy. "And I am not!"

Colin frowned. "Is so. I've played it online, on emulators."

"Then, you'd be mistaken, young man," I intoned matter-of-factly, adopting my fake British accent. "Now, if the young Master would care to add '2084' to the end of it, I would be inclined to believe you."

Colin gasped with surprise.

"Struck a chord, I think I have," I continued, which made Colin chuckle. "Tell you what, you impetuous boy. I hereby challenge you to a Robotron 2084 throw down. That game, and many others, are currently on my arcade cabinet back in my place. Wouldeth thou careth to undertaketh the challenge?"

Colin was snorting with laughter. "I will wipe the floor with you, old man."

"Old man, he says," I drawled, as I slapped a hand over my heart. "As my generation used to say, 'It's on like ...'"

"... Donkey Kong!" Colin finished for me. "Can you really play Robotron at your house?"

I nodded. "Yep. I was about to invite you and your mother to come over to our place for Thanksgiving, since we aren't going anywhere this year. I just have to get your mom to agree."

The boy's expression sobered. "Grandma has been pushing us to come visit for the week. I know Mom wants to, but we can't."

"So, you'll be here in town. Good. You'll be here for your butt whoopin'. Glad to hear it. I'll take care of your mom."

Colin chuckled again and nodded.

"Hey, would you do me a favor? Would you watch the dogs for me? I have to track down Jillian before she buys everything in the store."

Colin laughed and held out a hand. I passed him the leashes, but not before I noticed Sherlock perking up. He and Watson both stared up at the boy and cocked their heads, something I haven't seen them do to him before. I was about to ask Colin if he had recently eaten, which means he could've spilled something on himself (which could account for the dogs' sudden fascination with him) when the boy shut off his tablet. He pulled his backpack from somewhere behind the counter and slid his computer inside.

The two corgis only had eyes for the tablet, it would seem. No, correct that. It looked like they were staring at the backpack. Why? What was in it? As I walked away and thanked my corgi-sitter, I quickly pulled out my phone and snapped a shot of Colin's bag before I lost sight of him.

When I found the girls, they were in the middle of a hushed conversation. Hmm, let's change that to *argument*. From the look of things, Jillian was trying to talk Hannah into doing something, and Hannah was flat-out refusing. And, much to her credit, she wasn't backing down.

"Everything all right over here?" I asked, using the friendliest tone I could muster. "Is there anything I can do?"

"We're good, Zachary. In fact, Hannah and Colin have agreed to join us for Thanksgiving!"

Hannah smiled fleetingly at me before the tiniest bit of a scowl appeared on her face. And that was only when she glanced at Jillian. There was definitely something amiss, but seeing how I wasn't the one the girls were mad at, I decided to leave it alone unless I was asked to give an opinion.

"Cool! We're going to have fun! I have a new arcade machine that I've been itching to show Colin. He just told me he enjoyed playing the old retro arcade games like Pac-Man, Donkey Kong, and Frogger. I promptly challenged him to a game of Robotron, which he seems to think he'll win. Well, boy howdy, is he gonna get his rump kicked."

That brought a much-needed smile from Hannah, which was what I had been striving to do.

"I don't know, Zachary. I've seen Colin play those games. He's pretty good."

"I don't think you understand just how big of a nerd Zachary really is," Jillian said, laughing. "I've seen him play those games. There are some he's really good at."

The smile melted from my face. "Some? Some? Lady, I'm good at them *all*."

"Tetris," Jillian immediately responded.

I crossed my arms over my chest. "Tetris isn't an arcade game."

"Sure, it is," Jillian argued.

"Believe it or not, it is," Hannah agreed. "It was in the arcades long before the Gameboy ever came around."

"And you know this *how*?" I suspiciously asked.

"Because I was the Queen of Tetris," Hannah

proudly stated. "No one could beat me."

"And Super Mario Brothers 2?" Jillian coyly asked.

"Aww, come on!" I complained. "That one is definitely not an arcade game. I can only play it on my cabinet because I set it up that way."

"You still lost," Jillian teased. She winked at Hannah, which caused her to giggle. "It really wasn't much of a contest."

"Okay, fine," I groused. "Statement amended to say, 'I'm good at *most* of the games.' There, better?"

Jillian nodded, pleased. "That'll do. So, Hannah, this get-together we're having on Thanksgiving? I need some decorations."

"First, tell me what I can bring," Hannah implored.

Jillian was already shaking her head. However, that's when I saw the frown reappear on Hannah's face. Suddenly deducing that the source of anxiety between my fiancée and Hannah was financially motivated, I decided to step in.

"Tell me you know how to make butt rolls," I eagerly said, as I addressed Hannah. "I *love* those things."

The frown morphed into the beginnings of a smile. "Butt rolls? Are you serious?"

"Oh, yeah! They're fantastic. Taste so good, they don't even need butter."

Hannah curiously looked at Jillian and shrugged. "I'll make them if you tell me how."

Jillian had started smiling the moment I gave

Hannah the suggestion. "Sure. It's not nearly as hard as it sounds. Get a bag of frozen, uncooked rolls. Spray a cupcake tin—which I have a few if you need to borrow one—with cooking spray. Place two frozen rolls in each cupcake tin. Cover with a piece of plastic wrap, but I would suggest spraying it with cooking spray, too. Let them thaw, which will make them rise, and voila! Butt rolls. Although, for the record, I think they should be called something else besides that."

"Then why call them that at all?" Hannah asked, as she turned back to me.

"You tell me what those rolls look like to you once they've risen," I snickered. "You won't call them anything else."

"Butt rolls," Hannah chortled. "Only you, Zack. Okay, you need some harvest-themed decorations? Let me show you what I have."

Jillian's phone rang right then. I watched her glance at the display and, before I knew what was happening, cringe. Curiosity piqued, I sidled closer, only Jillian planted a hand on my chest, shook her head, and then inclined it in Hannah's direction. The meaning came through loud and clear. Whatever the reason for the call, she needed to take it in a quiet place. So, she wanted me to pick out some appropriate décor.

"I need to take this," Jillian apologized, as she hurried out of the store.

"Is everything okay?" Hannah sounded worried. "I don't usually see Jillian get worked up like that."

"I'm sure it'll be fine," I assured her. "So, what decorations do you have that are Thanksgiving-themed?"

Shrugging, Hannah turned and led me deeper into her store. She took me to a display stand, and on it was an arrangement with a wide vase, a variety of orange flowers and red berries.

"This one, for example, has several mini pumpkins, as you can see," Hannah was saying. "I've incorporated a few orange roses, orange carnations, some chrysanthemums, and even a few red currants. Oh, do you see those? Those are poppies."

"Very festive," I said, as I studied the arrangement. "Love the colors. We'll take it."

"You will? It's kinda expensive, Zack. But, I can give you a manager's discount. I ..."

"You'll do nothing of the sort," I scoffed. "If you give me free stuff, then I'll do the same to you. Now, what about that? It looks like some type of wreath?"

Hannah nodded as she pulled a step stool out from behind a large rack and gingerly pulled the wreath from the wall.

"I wove grapevines together to get the overall shape, and then incorporated ... let me guess. You don't care, do you?"

I grinned and shoved my hands in my pockets. "Guilty as charged. It has those little mini pumpkins on it, and that's all it needs to get my vote. I think it looks nice. I'll take that one, too."

As I followed Hannah to the front of the store, we passed by a worn, walnut bureau, which was being used to display multiple knick-knacks Hannah had for sale. I caught sight of a set of hand-carved, wooden pumpkins, which had a small cut-out to place a name card. That was something, I decided, Jillian would love: pumpkin name card holders. There were six pumpkins in each set, and there were three sets available for sale.

I took all three.

Jillian returned from her call in time to see me presenting my credit card to pay for the purchases. She sidled up next to me, slipped her arm through mine, and leaned against my side. Thanking Hannah profusely for her help, we headed outside with the first load of purchases. Once there, Jillian began giggling.

"Is everything okay?" I worriedly asked. "For some reason, I thought you'd be more concerned than this. You're laughing? Curiosity has been piqued. What's up?"

Jillian took a deep breath, held it for a few moments, and then slowly let it out. She faced Hannah, smiled, and then looked at me.

"That was Julie. She, uh, received some news today that she's pretty sure is going to freak out Harrison."

"I hope she's okay," Hannah worriedly said.

Julie was the wife of my best friend from high school, Harrison Watt. How both of us started in Phoenix, Arizona, only to end up in Pomme Valley, Oregon, continued to amaze me. And Julie, I might add, was currently pregnant with her third child. That was a fact that originally didn't go over well with Harry, who automatically assumed he wasn't the father, and ... let's just say things went downhill from there. Fast.

That's all in the past now. The last I heard, everyone was happy. So, what had happened? What piece of news had Julie just passed on to Jillian?

"They're having twins!" Jillian excitedly announced. "She went in for an ultrasound today, and the doctor confirmed there were multiple heartbeats. Can you believe it, Zachary?"

"Harry is gonna freak," I chortled. "What did he end up saying?"

"She hasn't told him yet. That's why she called me. She was certain Harrison was going to react badly to the news, but I managed to talk her down. Harrison would never treat her that way."

"At least, not on purpose," I added. I looked over at Jillian's friend, who had returned to the front counter. "They'll be fine. Hey, if you don't mind me asking, is everything all right with Hannah? When I came back from chatting with Colin, I saw the two of you in the midst of a hushed conversation. You were exasperated, and Hannah was angry. Wait, not angry. Defiant."

She gave me an amazed look. "I'm impressed. That's exactly what was going through Hannah's head--defiance. Things are tight with her and

Colin this year, and seeing how I didn't want to see anyone hurting, I offered a small loan."

"She refused," I guessed.

Jillian nodded. "To put it bluntly, yes. I'm hoping I can talk her into accepting it. At the very least, she and Colin will be celebrating Thanksgiving with us. So, it sounds like you're getting along with Colin. I thought you told me you were uncomfortable around children?"

I shrugged. "What can I say? I like him. He's a smart kid. Quiet. I guess he reminds me of myself when I was that age. Plus, it turns out he loves vintage video games. Challenging me to an 80's video game throw down? I'm gonna dust the floor with him."

"You are going to lose to a 12-year-old," Jillian teased.

"Probably," I laughed.

It took several trips to the car to get everything (and everyone) properly loaded. Jillian took one look at the bag full of pumpkin place card holders and clapped excitedly, knowing full well she was already planning out how she was going to have her dinner table look. Then, came an unwelcome interruption...

"Oh my! We can fly! You can fly! We can fly! Come on, everybody, here we go!"

I ended up snorting with laughter before I was able to prevent my cell phone from repeating the new ringtone I had specifically picked out for my detective friend. What was it? Why, it was nothing more than the theme from Peter Pan. In case you want to know why that was so funny to me, check YouTube and look up tap-dancing detective!

"Zack? It's happened again. There's ... why are you laughing? Never mind. I need your help. Another grocery store has been hit!"

FOUR

As I pulled up to the latest grocery store that had been vandalized, which was El Gato Supermercado, located on the east side of Medford, several things became very apparent to me. First off, there was only one police cruiser parked outside the store. Was there so much crime happening in our neighboring city that Medford could only spare one police officer? And second, this store was about the same size as the grocery store that was hit a few days ago in Grants Pass. Coincidence?

The damage to this store wasn't nearly as severe as what had happened to Vicki's Grab & Go. There were no shattered windows, but the front door did look as though it had taken a mighty blow. The glass, I was told later, was safety glass, so it resisted shattering, but that didn't stop it from splintering. Hundreds of cracks snaked out in all directions, forming one mighty impressive-looking spider web. To me, it looked as though someone kicked their way through the front door, and instead of breaking the glass, the lock finally broke, allowing entry.

I spotted Vance's car next to the MPD cruiser and took the spot next to him. Helping their Royal Highnesses to the ground, the dogs and I turned to face the store, as if each of us was doing the same thing, namely trying to determine why this particular store was struck. The front door opened and Vance waved us in.

"Hey, Zack. Glad you're here. And there's Sherlock and Watson, my two favorite Dog Wonders. I've got something for you both."

Two corgi derrieres immediately sat, with the nubs of their tails wagging like crazy. As the dogs munched on their biscuits, I watched two police officers—one was a tall, middle-aged woman and the other a young guy—exit the store, catch sight of Vance squatting next to the dogs, and amble over. The female cop then noticed the dogs and a huge smile split her face.

"It's Sherlock and Watson! I remember you two adorable fluffballs!"

If anything could make the corgis abandon Vance and his seemingly unending supply of biscuits, then it'd be an enthusiastic greeting from someone new. Sherlock quickly rose to his feet and trotted over, followed immediately by Watson. The officer squatted low and, just like that, both dogs went belly-up.

"You've met them before?" I asked, as I approached the two Medford officers.

JEFFREY POOLE

The woman nodded. "It must've been a few years ago. I believe you were investigating a series of dognappings, weren't you?

I nodded. "Good memory. We were looking for connections for a rash of dognappings that happened here in Medford a while ago. Vance brought us over and introduced us to everyone."

"The dogs were a hit," the officer confirmed. She straightened and held out a hand. "I'm Officer Danielle Hartman. This is my partner, Officer Richard Montoyo."

Having already met, Vance made the introductions for us, and even elicited a chuckle from Officer Montoyo when he included the dogs.

"What's it look like in there?" I wanted to know.

"I personally think this was nothing but a group of teenagers, looking to steal some booze."

"The pharmacy wasn't hit?" I asked.

Both officers shook their heads.

"El Gato Supermercado," Officer Montoyo explained, "if you couldn't tell by the name, is a Mexican supermarket. They're not big, but they are local favorites. Plus, they don't have a pharmacy in there."

Remembering that the pharmacy wasn't the only part of the Grants Pass store to get hit, I turned to Vance. "Was there any other part of the store that was targeted?"

"There are tipped over racks and we found some products knocked from shelves," Officer

88

Hartman answered. "Trust me, guys, as much as I love having Sherlock and Watson here, this was just the result of some dimwitted teenagers."

"What kind of booze was taken?" Vance wanted to know.

"Beer," Officer Montoyo replied. "Nearly a dozen cases."

I looked at Vance. "Think there are any dumpsters nearby?"

"Why do you ask that?" Officer Hartman wanted to know.

"Did you hear about the store that was hit in Grants Pass?" Vance asked.

Both officers nodded. After all, these were all small towns in the grand scheme of things.

"Well, their pharmacy was hit, but Sherlock and Watson found the stolen drugs in a dumpster less than a mile away."

"They ditched the drugs?" Officer Montoyo asked, puzzled. "That doesn't make any sense."

"We know," Vance agreed. "So, when my partner here asked if there were any nearby dumpsters ..."

"You think they might have dumped the booze, too?" Officer Hartman asked, after Vance had trailed off.

"That's the ongoing theory," Vance confirmed.

Officer Hartman shrugged. "Your Spanish is way better than mine. You stay here. I'll go take a look around."

Officer Montoyo nodded. "Yes, ma'am."

I looked at the front door. "Is this how they gained entry?"

Both Officer Montoyo *and* Vance shook their heads.

"No," my friend told me. He pointed at a narrow alley on the right. "There's a side door over there, and it looks as though it's been picked. There are fresh scratches on the lock."

I looked back at the heavily damaged front door. "Then, what's with the broken door? Why not just leave the same way they got in?"

Vance shrugged. "I don't have an answer to that. Perhaps ... perhaps we're dealing with the stupidest criminals ever?"

"Someone wants us to think this was how they got in," Officer Montoyo added. "But, anyone— professional or amateur—can see that this was *not* how they gained entry."

A full-sized, quad-cab pickup suddenly pulled up to the store. An elderly Hispanic couple emerged and headed straight to the two uniformed police officers. Perhaps they were the owners of the store?

Officer Montoyo stepped up and began speaking with them in Spanish. I knew Vance could speak the language, but judging from the look on his face, my detective friend wasn't able to follow along with this particular conversation. Why? Probably because they were speaking way too fast.

After a few minutes had passed, the conversation came to an end, and Officer Montoyo ushered us over.

"These are the owners of El Gato. Señor and Señora Olvidera."

We shook hands.

"Señor? Señora? This is the team from Pomme Valley, sent over to assist us. This is Detective Vance Samuelson and Zack Anderson, a police consultant. And ... down there? That one, the one with the black. He's Sherlock. The other one is Watson."

The woman smiled. "*¡Que bonita!*"

Mr. Olvidera took my hand and eagerly pumped it up and down. "Hola, Señor Anderson. I am told your dogs can help us locate who did this to our store?"

The woman's expression soured as she glanced up at the damaged front door. "*Pendejos. Quisiera mételes un chile por el culo.*"

Vance snorted with laughter while Mr. Olvidera's eyes widened with disbelief. The shop keeper hurriedly turned to his wife.

"*No hagas una escena. Me ocuparé de esto.* So, Señor Anderson, what do you need from me?"

I pointed at the two dogs. "Well, we'd like to take a look around, but this is a grocery store, and I'm guessing you typically don't allow animals in there? So, we'd need your permission to enter."

The store owner waved off our concerns. "Please. Look around. Anything you can do is fine with us."

Vance nodded. "Thank you, Mr. Olvidera. Zack? Let's go."

Vance gingerly opened the damaged door, stepped inside, and held it open for me and the dogs. As I stepped inside, and looked around, I was immediately reminded of the name of this particular store. It was in Spanish and the store owners were Mexican. That meant this store catered to the Hispanic community.

"What did they say?" I asked Vance, as soon as we were out of earshot.

"Hmm? Oh, the owners? Well, Mrs. Olvidera thought the dogs were both cute."

"Yeah, I figured that part out on my own. What did she say after that? She said something which made you laugh and made her husband blush."

"He was embarrassed. Let's just say she had a few choice words for the perps who did this, and she suggested a course of action should she ever encounter the person who did this face-to-face."

"Really? Come on, pal. Tell me what she really said."

"Fine. She said she wanted to shove a chili up their rears."

"Nice," I chuckled. "And appropriate."

We both ventured further inside. Officer Montoyo was right. This store catered to the Mexican community here in Medford. I don't know if you've ever been inside a Mexican store, or any type of establishment which carried only a specific type of product, but in my case, this was a first for me. Upon stepping inside, my eyes were drawn to the cleanliness of the store. Products were arranged tastefully. Floors were clean. There were bright, colorful banners everywhere, which were touting (I'm assuming) this week's specials. Then again, I could also see tipped over racks of greeting cards and several destroyed displays of what I'm guessing was candy.

I walked over to a display rack of tortilla chips. The bags looked like anything I'd expect to find back at Gary's Grocery, only everything was in Spanish. Name, description, calorie counts, and ingredients, all were in Spanish.

One thing I noticed right off the bat was that the products definitely had more flavors. By that, I mean everything looked really spicy. And it was at this exact moment when I remembered my friend, Harry, still owed me a dinner. He and I, while we were in Monterey, had made a wager where the loser would have to do the other's bidding. Harry, the little schmuck, had hoped I'd have to scrub some of his kennels at his office. Seeing how he ran the town's veterinary clinic, and also ran a rescue shelter to find 'furever' homes for the animals that were brought to him, he was always needing his kennels thoroughly cleaned. Thankfully, I had won the wager, and Harry had agreed to go to dinner with me and eat anything I picked out for him. In case you're wondering, this was a direct retaliation for him giving me hell for accidentally ordering frog legs at Jillian's favorite restaurant.

Yes, I *did* try them, in order to save face with Jillian, and no, they did *not* taste like chicken.

So, I've been waiting for the right opportunity to spring my surprise on my unsuspecting friend. Looking at the flavors before me, and the many choices of hot sauces lining the shelves, I made a mental note to go shopping afterward and, more than likely, enlist the help of my new friend here. I just had to make sure to record the entire ordeal. It was time someone dethroned Vance as the most popular YouTuber living in Pomme Valley.

The leashes went taut. Glancing down, I could see that both Sherlock and Watson wanted to head toward the produce department. Looking behind me to verify Vance was there, which he was, we moved to the right and headed toward El Gato's selection of fruit and vegetables. Sherlock stopped at a display of plastic boxes of strawberries, like the kind you find at any other store, and stared for a few moments.

I pulled out my cell and was ready to take a picture when Sherlock was off again. This time, he stopped at a display of small, orange peppers whose points tapered to a tip. I picked one up to give it a cursory sniff.

My eyes widened with surprise and I'm pretty sure I lost all the skin cells on the inside of my nose. Holy cow. Why did I get the impression that, if I strayed too close to these peppers, that I was going to melt my eyebrows off? There was a snowball's chance in hell I would be able to eat that. I thought of Harry, and a huge grin appeared on my face.

Oh, I was going to have some fun in this store.

Convinced there was nothing worthy of their attention, the dogs pulled me over to another section of the produce area. This one had berries. Strawberries, to be exact. Carton after carton of strawberries were neatly stacked on a table, with a sign offering a price of $2 per carton.

"They look good, don't they?" I quietly told the dogs. "I think we're going to have to go shopping here once we're all done. Now, what are we looking at?"

The dogs sidled closer to the strawberries, but damned if they didn't look as if they were trying to see up and into the display. Maybe they wanted to know what was next to them? Approaching the display stand, I leaned over the lip of the table to see for myself what was there. And the answer?

Nothing.

By that, I meant there was an empty, narrow space to the left of the strawberries. Peering closely at the price tag beneath the empty bin, I could make out a few words.

"What is 'arándano rojo'?" I asked.

Vance thought for a moment. "Well, 'rojo' is 'red', and 'arándano'? I'm not sure. It's some type of berry, I think. Officer Montoyo? Could you come here a second? What does that say?"

The young Hispanic officer squatted next to the price tag and scanned the print. "Cranberry.

Well, it'd be 'red cranberry', if you want to get technical."

That's just my luck. They're out of cranberries, too? I was really hoping I could find some in here and surprise Jillian with a bag or two. What the hell was going on lately, anyway? Was there a shortage of these things?

The dogs and I skirted an assortment of canned vegetables on the ground. The more I looked, the more I noticed the disarray left behind by the perp. Or perps, I guess. Maybe the Medford cops were right. Maybe these two incidents weren't related after all?

Sherlock and Watson now led us to the right, which was where we could see a narrow door with the word Emergencia stenciled in red across the front. You didn't need to be fluent in the language to figure out the purpose of that door. I nudged Vance and pointed at the exit.

"Can you tell if that door is alarmed? If that's where the perp entered, wouldn't he have set off an alarm in doing so?"

Vance stepped up to the door and ran his fingertips along the edges. "There was no mention of an alarm being tripped. Hey, Officer Montoyo? Can you ask the Olvideras if this door has an alarm on it?"

The officer nodded and hurried outside.

"Think it does?" I quietly asked.

"What, have an alarm? It doesn't look like it. Otherwise, if it does, and since no alarm was reported, I'd have to upgrade our perp from novice to someone who knows what they're doing."

"That's a no," Officer Montoyo called from the front door.

"Thank you," Vance called back. "No alarm, that's good. Let's take a look at the lock." My detective friend pushed open the door and then squatted low to inspect the exterior door handle. After a few moments, he pulled out a pen and tapped the keyhole. "Yep, you can see it right here. See these scratches? Those are made from picks. This lock was picked, all right, but it was definitely done by an amateur."

I'd encountered this before, along with the ways you can tell a pro job from an amateur, on a previous case. I nodded. "Got it. All right, this is our entry-point. Sherlock? Watson? Did you want to …"

I trailed off as the dogs made for the other side of the store. Where did we end up? At a hardware/houseware aisle. This store has a small section of products for DIY'ers: screws, nails, a few extension cords, and the like. The corgis pulled me over to a small section of hanging letters and numbers. These, I noted, were what you'd use if you wanted to put your address on your mailbox, or maybe on the side of your house. Oddly enough, there must have been a run on this particular section, because nearly half the choices were gone. Whatever. As for the dogs? Well, they were staring at the numbers, specifically the lone numeral 7, hanging by itself on its peg.

"What are we looking at?" Vance wanted to know, as he came up behind me.

I pointed at the dangling number. "You tell me. Does 7 mean anything to you?"

"Nope."

I pulled out my cell and took a picture. "Roger that. I'm right there with you. Guys? Care to indicate what we're supposed to do with this?"

Sherlock snorted once, looked at his pack-mate, and promptly headed back.

"Didn't we just come from this way?" Vance quietly asked.

I was about ready to agree, only we veered at the last minute and headed to a set of swinging doors, which led to the produce department's back room. Once the four of us were standing in the quiet workroom, Vance and I shared a look. Neither of us could see anything out of place back here.

Counters were clean. Floors were swept and spotless. Knives and tools were hanging on their respective hooks. Several dozen boxes (of varying sizes) were stacked against the far wall, waiting to be flattened.

"Looks fine to me," Vance decided.

Sherlock dropped his nose to the floor, sniffed a few times, and then headed for the closest cabinet. There, on the ground, just under the lip of the counter, was some type of fruit. Something small, and something round. Blueberry? Cherry?

I squatted down and gingerly slid my hand into the space between the counter and the floor. It was a berry, all right, only—you guessed it—it was a cranberry!

Rising to my feet, I held my find out for Vance's approval.

"What do you have there? Is that a cranberry?"

"Remember what was stolen from the freezer back in Grants Pass?"

Vance was silent as he considered. "Boxes of these things, right?"

I hooked a thumb at the displays on the other side of the store. "Remember that cranberry section? They were out, too. Coincidence?"

"Zack, I sincerely doubt that particular cranberry is related to this break-in."

"Oh, come on! Of course it is! Think about it. No cranberries at Gary's Grocery. That store in Grants Pass was out, and now this one? It's too coincidental."

"I'm guessing that thing has been under the counter for at least two weeks or so."

I stared at the red berry in my hand. "How could you possibly know that?"

"I'm going off the green mold that's on the backside of that berry."

My hand sprang open, as though I had suddenly discovered I was holding a live spider.

"Oh, ewww! That's nasty! Why didn't you say something?"

"I *did* say something, pal. Hey, I could've left

you holding it, but did I? No. I was nice enough to ... don't even think about wiping that hand on me."

It must have been the tone of our voices. The dogs sensed that Vance and I were horsing around, so naturally, they wanted to be included. Sherlock let out an eardrum-shattering bark. The only thing Watson did was whine but to be honest, I'm guessing. The ringing in my ears was so bad that I only *thought* I could hear her.

"Wow. That was loud, pal. Here. We're okay. Have a biscuit."

Once both corgis had devoured their second treat of the day, they were off. Again. This time, we were following a narrow hallway which, I'm guessing, would connect us to the main storeroom in the back. A few moments later, my suspicions were confirmed.

"Do all grocery stores have these hidden passageways?" Vance curiously asked, as we emerged into the large storeroom.

I shrugged. "I wouldn't call 'em 'hidden'. I would imagine the employees need a way to get around without being seen, or getting in the way of the customers."

We heard a loud clatter from somewhere to the left, out of sight. Both corgis woofed a warning, and Vance's hand automatically dropped to his hip, to land on the butt of his gun.

"Vance Samuelson, Pomme Valley PD. Who's there? Identify yourself."

"This is a Mexican store," I quietly reminded my friend.

"Oh, that's right. Uh, let me think. *Este es Vance Samuelson, de la policia. ¿Quién está ahí?*"

A young boy, whom I was guessing was in his mid-teens, wearing a bright green apron, appeared. The boy held his hands high in the air as he cautiously edged out into the open.

"Don't shoot!" the young clerk cried, in perfect English. "I work here!"

"What are you doing in here, kid?" Vance wanted to know. "This is a crime scene. Didn't you know this place was burglarized?"

The teenager nodded. "I did, yes. That's why I'm here. I'm trying to clean up. It's my job to keep this area free of debris at all times. I was just trying to help."

I heard a whine and immediately glanced at the dogs. Both corgis were looking at the large swinging doors, leading out into the store.

Vance looked angrily around at the backroom and then locked eyes on the nervous teen.

"You've tampered with a crime scene. Damn! We needed to see what it looked like in here. I should charge you with …"

I nudged my friend's shoulder. "He's about to pee himself, pal. Getting angry with him isn't gonna solve anything." Looking at the frightened kid, I raised my voice. "What's your name?"

"Enrique. Enrique Corona. Am I going to be arrested?"

I looked over at Vance, who had an expression on his face which said he was seriously considering it.

I snapped my fingers a few times to get the kid's attention. "Enrique? Listen to me very carefully. This is important. We need to know what type of mess you discovered back here? What have you had to clean up?"

Enrique pointed at a stack of boxes near the door.

"Those were tipped over. And fruit. There was some fruit on the ground."

"From the break-in?" Vance asked, as his eyes dropped to the floor. "Do you usually find discarded fruit on the floor in here?"

I pointed back at the way we had come. "Produce is *that* way. What would … forget about that. Let me ask this: what fruit did you find?"

Enrique shrugged and pointed at an open trash receptacle, the kind which are normally found at the end of the street on trash days. I would also like to point out that the large green trash bin was situated just inside the backroom, next to the doors. It would seem the dogs had been staring at the trash can rather than the door.

Vance pulled out a small flashlight and shone it into the bin. He grunted, pulled out his cell, and snapped a few pics. Then, he motioned me over.

"What is it?" I wanted to know.

"See for yourself."

Leaning over, I glanced in the bin. There, visible amidst the rather large dust bunnies and small piles of dust, were several round objects. Surprised, I looked back at my friend.

"Are those ...?"

"Cranberries," Vance confirmed.

We both looked down at the dogs. Sherlock's smirk was back, while Watson wriggled with excitement. How could they have known to look in there? I pulled out my own cell and took a few pictures.

"There's something about these cranberries," Vance grumbled. "What the hell am I missing? Who would steal cranberries, especially at this time of year?" Vance's cell chose that time to ring. Glancing down, he cringed. "It's the captain. I've gotta take this. Are you good here? I'll be just outside."

"We're fine. Go."

Once Vance was gone, I returned my gaze to the trash can and focused on the discarded berries. Why would someone be stealing all the cranberries? Did someone hate them that badly?

I looked over at the teenager. "Enrique? By any chance, do you have any more cranberries in stock? Fresh or frozen, it doesn't matter to me."

"I do not think so, but I will check for you."

The clerk ducked into the long, narrow hallway leading to the produce department.

"Wouldn't it be nice to surprise Jillian with some cranberries?" I asked the dogs. "She's worried she won't be able to find any, and I have to say,

I'm starting to worry a little, too. I mean, have you guys ever heard about anything as bizarre as this?"

Sherlock and Watson ignored me. In fact, Sherlock slid into a 'down' position, but before he could nod off, Enrique was back. He looked at me and shook his head.

"There are no fresh cranberries, it would seem."

"Oh, man," I sighed. "Well, what about frozen?"

Enrique nodded, and stepped up to the thick metal door leading into the walk-in freezer. Steeling himself, the teenager yanked the door open and ducked inside. Frosty, super-chilled air spilled out, causing the dogs to both shake their coats and retreat to my side.

"It's a wee bit chilly in there, isn't it?" I told the dogs. "That's why I wouldn't let you go in the other freezer in Grants Pass. It's not for corgis, I'm sorry to say."

Enrique emerged and hastily closed the freezer door. He rubbed his hands together and then blew on them, presumably to warm them up.

"Any luck?" I asked.

Enrique shook his head. "I don't understand. There were two cases of frozen berries in there from last night's delivery. We rarely go through them, but for this time of year, we do stock up."

Vance returned just then, in time to hear the part about the missing holiday favorites.

"We have another store with stolen cranberries? What are the odds of that?"

"Do you think that's what the perp was after?" I asked.

"Someone went to all this effort just to steal a few boxes of cranberries? Come on, Zack. That's a stretch, even for you."

"The facts fit the crime," I pointed out.

"Nobody steals cranberries," Vance insisted.

"Well, it sure seems that way," I argued. "There are none in PV, the store we were at in Grants Pass was out, and now this one. What other conclusions are we supposed to come to?"

"There's a logical explanation. There has to be. What, do you think our perp is going to hold these cranberries for ransom?"

"He could," I scoffed.

To help prove my point, Sherlock chose that time to let out a snort. A loud one. Grinning, I ruffled his fur.

"All right, let's go. Has either of the dogs stopped at anything else?"

I shrugged. "Let's find out."

And the answer to that would be a resounding no. We walked up and down every single aisle in that store. We then headed outside and checked the perimeter of the building. Twice. Did the dogs smell anything? Did they show any signs of interest?

Nope.

Whatever we were meant to learn was confined to the inside, with the exception of the side door. Sherlock and Watson both glanced up at it as we passed. Both times. I can only assume that, since they already alerted us to the door the one time, a second inspection was unnecessary.

It wasn't until thirty minutes later, when the both of us decided to head back to Pomme Valley, that I got word from Vance: the stolen booze had been located in an abandoned car, located less than a mile away.

"What do you think it means?" I asked.

"Personally? I think these burglaries are just diversionary tactics. Someone thinks they're throwing us off the scent by perpetuating these other crimes."

"And doing a terrible job at it," I added. "If you're going to just dump the loot you've stolen, then you'd think they'd find a better location."

"Right? Thus far, I think the real target has been the freezers."

"You're referring to the cranberries, aren't you? So, you believe me now?"

"It feels strange as hell to say this, but I think someone wants all the cranberries. So, yes, you're making a believer out of me. We just have to figure out why. Why aren't the other stores being targeted? Why only these two? How are these two facilities linked?"

FIVE

Didn't we already do this? I mean, you and I both fought back the crowds a few days ago. Now, here we are—again—at the grocery store. From the looks of things, it's even worse *now* than it was *then*."

Jillian nodded. "I know, right? But, what choice have we? I don't want to wait for the last possible moment to get the supplies we need. I'm still missing a few things, so here we are."

"Would you like a cart?"

"Yes, please."

"Where to first?"

"Let's see if they have any cranberries first. That's what I'd like to get my hands on the most."

"Roger that. Wow, I can't believe how many people are in here. Granted, Thanksgiving is less than a week away, but … Jillian? I'm sorry to tell you this, but it looks like they're still out of fresh cranberries."

"Oh, rats. Well, maybe they were able to re-stock the frozen variety?"

I hurried over to the freezers and stared at the empty spot on the shelf. Nope. If Gary's had received another shipment, then we were shi ... er, make that *completely* out of luck. Jillian was going to have to figure out something else she could use.

"Nothing?" Jillian sighed, as she eyed my empty arms. "I can't believe they're still out of cranberries."

"Can you use anything else? Like a substitute, perhaps?"

"I'll have to think about it. I may have to call Taylor and ask her for some advice."

"Well, she *is* the baker," I reminded her. I caught sight of a couple of brand new empty flats, next to the cranberry bin, and pointed at it. "What gives? Those weren't out earlier. I wonder what was in there?"

Jillian leaned forward. "Blueberries. It says blueberries, Zachary. Why would they be out?"

"Why would cranberries?" I countered.

Jillian nodded. "A fair question. This is just strange. I've never seen a run on *anything* at the grocery store before. Come on. I want to check the frozen section. Maybe we'll get lucky and find a bag or two of cranberries there."

A family rushed by us a few moments later, pushing two carts laden with food, toiletries, cleaning supplies, and so on. I didn't really pay any attention to it, nor did Jillian. The only thing on my fiancée's mind was the procurement of cranberries, so she could make some of her favorite seasonal recipes. As for me, the only thing on my mind was *eating* those seasonal recipes.

Pushing our cart, I decided to swing by the frozen section a second time, this time with another set of eyes, just in case I might've missed something. Sadly, I hadn't. In fact, there were shelves in this freezer that were looking just as bare as the fresh berries section. Just what the hell was going on? What, were we in the middle of some type of pandemic? Just because a couple of grocery stores were vandalized, did that mean people should immediately begin hoarding supplies? Was that what the family with two carts was doing? Stocking up in case it was the end of the world?

"I don't understand what's going on here," Jillian quietly lamented. "All I need is a bag or two of cranberries."

"Unless the population of Pomme Valley has somehow increased without anyone else realizing it," I slowly began, "I can only assume the general public are freaking out for no reason. Did you see the canned goods aisle? Black beans were out. Beans! Who the hell would think to themselves, 'Dude, we can't run out of beans, bro! Buy 'em all!' It's ridiculous."

Jillian was laughing. "You sounded just like Harry!"

A young courtesy clerk wandered by at that moment.

"Hey!" I exclaimed. "Excuse me, could we ask

you a question?"

The clerk hastily back stepped until he was standing in front of us.

"Yes? Can I help you?'

I pointed at the freezer. "By any chance, do you have any more bags of cranberries back there?"

The teenager sighed and shook his head. "We've had everyone asking about them. We're out, I'm afraid. They were the first to go when the newspaper reported several other stores had their supplies stolen."

"And blueberries?" I continued. "And black beans? What's going on around here, anyway?"

The kid looked left, then right, as if he was afraid of being overheard.

"I know, right? This is insane. We haven't been this busy since ... *ever*. It's like every single person coming through the line has a minimum of $150 in groceries."

"People are buying things they don't need," Jillian sighed. "They're ..."

"... panic-buying," the clerk finished for her. "You're right. Aside from cranberries, do you have everything you need? Perhaps there's something you can't find that we might still have on the shelf?"

Another fully laden cart was pushed by us.

"I give it another 48 hours before you're going to be sold out of everything," I quietly deduced.

The clerk confidently shook his head. "There might be panic-buying happening in here, but the demand hasn't gone up. We've got another shipment coming in sometime in the next day or so. I know they were trying to push the delivery earlier, but I don't think that'll happen. Besides, I overheard my boss saying that there should be a shipment of cranberries included with that delivery."

"I'm very glad to hear it," Jillian told the boy. She pulled out her phone and checked the list she had digitally created. "How are your supplies of stuffing and gravy?"

The kid smiled. "I just walked down that aisle. I wouldn't want to create a panic, but we're good. And gravy? I saw both jars and cans."

I grinned and gave the kid a friendly slap on the shoulder. "Perfect."

"What about chopped pecans?" Jillian inquired. "I can't find those."

The clerk nodded. "How much do you need?"

"Just one bag, thank you."

"It's okay to tell her you're completely out," I offered.

"I'm making those sweet potatoes," Jillian sternly told me.

The teen grinned. "Sweet potatoes? With pecan topping? Sign me up! I'll get you a bag."

Jillian smiled at the boy, while casting a frown in my direction. "Thank you." The clerk hurried off. "You said you were going to try my recipe. There's no backing down now, Zachary."

"Yeah, yeah," I sighed. "What can I say? I took a

shot. It didn't pan out."

Jillian swatted my arm and pointed back toward the canned goods section.

"We need a can of olives. I have this recipe where ... what's with that face? Oh, don't tell me. You don't like olives."

"Umm, I'm not a fan."

"You know what I'm going to ask next, don't you?"

I grinned and nodded. "Yep. You're going to ask me if I've ever tried them. Well, I have. And, believe it or not, I didn't find the flavor truly distasteful, just unpleasant."

"Does that mean you'd be willing to try one of my famous stuffed olives?" Jillian asked.

"Tell you what. As long as you're okay if you hear me say, I truly didn't care for it, then I'll give it a try. I'm fairly certain I won't care for the taste, but I will try it. For you."

Jillian smiled. "That's what I wanted to hear. What I don't want to hear, however, is that I won't be able to make my grandmother's cranberry persimmons cookies. I've made those cookies every year since I was 14, and I have no intention of breaking that record."

"You'll be able to make your cookies," I vowed. "Even if it means I have to drive to Portland to buy a bag of cranberries. I just have one question."

"That's very sweet of you," Jillian gushed. "What's your question?"

"What's a persimmons? Is it a type of fruit?"

"You've never tried a persimmon before?"

"I think we've established I'm culinary-re-tarded," I reminded my fiancée.

Jillian giggled. "Well, you're right. It's a fruit."

"What's it taste like?" I curiously asked. "I've heard the name before, of course, but I have no idea what they look like or taste like."

"Let's see. Let me think how I should best describe them."

Jillian, master cook and owner of a cook book shop, had to think about how to best describe a persimmon? Why do I get a feeling that my red flags are about to go up? I have a bad feeling about this.

"There are no comparisons to any other fruit that I can think of," Jillian admitted. Just then, she snapped her fingers. "Ah, I've got it. Imagine, if you will, a mango and a roasted sweet pepper met up, fell in love, and had a baby. Now, dust that baby with a touch of cinnamon and presto, you have a persimmon."

"Mango and a roasted sweet pepper?" I repeated, with mock horror. "I've had mango, and while it's not a favorite, I can choke it down. Sweet peppers? Definitely not a fan, so I can't begin to imagine what a mixture of those two would taste like."

"You told me you'd try those cookies, too," Jillian reminded me. "Your mother tells me you love cookies. Any cookies. Trust me, you're going to love them!"

As we roamed around the store, picking up only what we needed, mind you, my mind started to wander. Why would a simple theft of cranberries create such panic as what we were experiencing today? For that matter, what in the world would someone want with that many cranberries?

"Can you imagine what would happen to Gary's Grocery if it was hit by the same thief who hit the other two?" Jillian quietly mused.

I swept an arm around the hustle and bustle of Pomme Valley's main grocery store, as tiny as it was.

"I'd rather not, thanks," I remarked.

"Penny for your thoughts?" Jillian suggested, as she found the canned olives and selected several varieties.

"Just now? I was wondering what schmuck, in his right mind, would want to steal a bunch of cranberries? I mean, aside from causing pandemonium at Ye Olde General Store, what's the purpose? Why go through all of this?"

"If I didn't know any better," Jillian began, as she moved to the canned vegetable section, "then I'd say they were looking for something."

"And they found it," I confirmed. "More frozen cranberries."

"No, you silly man. Let's say that this thief has hidden something with the cranberries. Or, more likely, there's something hidden inside the shipping box of cranberries."

"That's been sitting inside a freezer?" I asked, skeptically. "Can you give me an example?"

Jillian shrugged and lowered her voice. "What about drugs? What if, as the authorities were closing in, this thief had to hide a bag of drugs? And, if by some miracle, they were walking past a box ready to be shipped? What if it was dropped inside?"

"That's a mighty big 'what if'," I pointed out. "And cranberries? I don't think you can just leave an open box of cranberries—bound for a grocery store—at the local post office."

"It's a far-fetched suggestion," Jillian admitted. "I was just trying to come up with an explanation to fit the facts."

"It's a good idea," I decided.

"Do you really think so?" Jillian asked.

"Well, think about it. So far, the common denominator between the two break-ins are the cranberries. Both were stolen and not recovered, I might add."

"Yet, the pills and the booze *were* recovered from those two burglaries," Jillian reminded me.

"True. I'm not sure how that helps us, but I know it must mean something. How's your list coming along? Aside from cranberries, do you have everything?"

"We still need the ..."

The young clerk reappeared just then. He saw me watching and tossed a bag of *something* he was holding. Was it pasta?

I caught the item and then looked at my hand and groaned. Chopped pecans. Jillian was going to be able to make her blasted sweet potatoes. Don't get me wrong, it's not that I hate sweet potatoes, but there's just something about the flavor I don't care for. I know what you're thinking. I *should* like them, due to the word 'sweet' being included in the name. On top of which, my own mother used to make a version of sweet potatoes that had some type of roasted marshmallows on top.

I still didn't care for them. Oh, well. These recipes clearly mean something to Jillian, and I wasn't about to be the dolt who rains on her parade. So, some compromising was in order. Regardless of how they tasted, I would eat my fair share. I just had to make sure I had a can of soda on hand.

"Have all grocery stores had their cranberries stolen?" Jillian suddenly asked.

"I'm not sure," I admitted. "I think it's just those two so far. Why do you ask?"

"Well, the bigger stores have more stock. If you really wanted to get your hands on some frozen cranberries, then I would think you'd target the bigger stores. There's an Albertson's, a Walmart, and even a Safeway in Medford. Were any of them hit?"

Jillian headed toward the bakery while I pulled out my phone and fired off a few questions via text to Vance. In less than two minutes, we had our answer. Vance had—apparently—wondered the same thing and sent off his own inquiries. He confirmed he had no idea why cranberries were targeted and, once I asked if only those two stores had been hit, he said he'd make a few calls.

Another 15 minutes passed before we had texts back from him.

Have already asked the same thing. Was waiting on several more Medford stores before answering, but their replies just came in.

I hurried over to Jillian, just as she selected a loaf of French bread, and showed her the phone.

Distributor has nearly two dozen stores checking inventory. 2 have reported their supplies have vanished. Cranberries only thing missing / unaccounted.

"Two more," Jillian breathed. "Are they smaller stores?"

I eagerly tapped out the question.

Yes. Looking into how stores are connected. Will keep you posted.

"Vance thinks something is fishy, too," Jillian decided. She waggled her phone and then slid it in her purse. "That's everything. Well, mostly everything. Ready to go?"

Another harried shopper rushed by us. And yes, before you ask, his cart was full, but this time, there were a few items in there which made me laugh.

"Zachary, did you see that man? He must have had a hundred rolls of toilet paper. All this because a few grocery stores were vandalized? I don't get it."

I spotted another shopper approaching. He looked to be younger than me, maybe mid-thirties, and had a seriously unhappy expression on his face. He noticed me looking his way and shrugged.

"Toilet paper?" I incredulously asked. "If you don't mind me asking, what's with all the TP? Am I missing something?"

"If there's gonna be a run on supplies," the stranger began, "then the last thing I want to worry about is whether or not I have enough, er, paper to finish the job."

I snorted with laughter. "You make it sound as though we're in the midst of a panic-inducing run on all supplies."

The guy pointed at the prizes in his cart. "You ought to grab some for yourself. You never know what will happen."

"We will *not* be panic-buying anything," I pointed out. "The only thing we need, which Gary's is currently out of, is cranberries."

The young man nodded knowingly. "You, too? I need that, and a few other things. Oh, well. Better safe than sorry."

Unfazed by my blasé response to his invitation to join the pandemonium, the shopper moved on.

"People are just ..."

"... stupid," Jillian finished for me, after I had trailed off. "The general public is easily frightened. The most we can do is not let ourselves panic-buy anything."

"Consider it done."

We returned to Jillian's house, Carnation Cottage. As we walked in the door, with our arms laden with our purchases, I noticed both of the corgis were up on the couch, laying Sphinx-like, in front of the television. Thanks to Jillian's suggestion, I tuned in to a free preview of some canine-enriching programming which promised to capture and hold your beloved dog's attention. I remember scoffing at the notion there was programming explicitly tailored for an animal. But, the moment I set the channel, both Sherlock and Watson, who had been in the process of jumping down to follow us to the door, turned to stare at the TV. What was the program showing? Simple: a procession of dogs, enjoying themselves in an outdoor park.

With the exception of sinking into down positions, neither dog had moved an inch.

"Well, I know what I'm signing up for, when I get back home," I chuckled.

Speaking of homes, I should point out that I've been spending a lot of time over at Jillian's house lately. In fact, I'm pretty sure I was spending more time *here* than *there*. Why? Well, I wanted to be wherever Jillian was, and I know she was more comfortable in her house. Plus, her house was easily twice the size of my own. Ideally, I'd love to have Jillian's house on my winery's acreage, but let's face it. That wasn't gonna happen.

Neither of us have addressed what the living arrangements will be after we get married. Will we live here, in one of PV's historic houses? Or, would we choose to live on my fifty acres of land?

If given a choice, then I think I would still love to live out in the country. However, Jillian loves her house, and unless I plan on renovating my house or possibly expanding it, then ...

Hmmm. Hold the phone, I think we have a winner! I could upgrade my house and give it some major renovations. The kitchen would need to undergo a huge makeover. Since Jillian loves to cook, I'd have to double the counter space, increase storage, replace appliances, and so on. It might be easier to just raze everything to the ground and start fresh, from scratch.

Wait, could I do that?

The thrum of a lawnmower suddenly erupted nearby. Mentally reminding myself to *quietly* look into the possibility of tearing my house down to begin anew, I patted both dogs on the head and looked out the window. A landscaper's truck, towing a large trailer loaded with a wide assortment of tools, was parked outside. I hadn't known Jillian had her own landscaper, but based on how nice everything looked, it really shouldn't be too surprising.

"You've got some people outside, working on your lawn," I called to Jillian.

Jillian rounded the corner and nodded. "Oh, good. I need to talk to them. I'm hoping they can trim back the pine tree closest to the house. It's getting too close for comfort, if you ask me."

The two of us headed for the front door. Sherlock and Watson finally tore themselves away from the TV and joined us. Clipping their leashes on, we headed outside and were instantly assailed by the exhaust from the lawnmower and the telltale scent of fresh grass clippings. One guy was busy raking up after the mower, and a second guy was loading the clippings into a wheelbarrow.

Also visible was a young boy of eight or nine, who was sitting on one of the porch steps. His head was down and he seemed to be staring at something in his lap. I'm guessing it was some type of electronic device?

I felt the leashes go taut. The dogs, it would seem, had noticed the youngster and were staring at him, as though they suspected he was hiding treats in his pockets. Moments later, I heard a few beeps and several synthesized explosions, confirming my guess the device was some type of video game. I tugged on the leashes, indicating my desire to follow Jillian as she headed for the guy currently raking the lawn. The dogs, however, refused to budge.

Sherlock looked at me, stretched, and then wiggled with excitement. Watson whined and pulled on her leash, too. Both dogs, it would seem, wanted to meet the boy. Upon seeing the dogs, the boy set his game on the step next to him, and stood up.

"Do you like dogs?" I asked the boy.

The kid emphatically nodded his head. I looked over at Jillian, for permission to allow an introduction. She was in the midst of a conversation with whom I'm guessing was the owner of the landscaping company, when she saw me looking her way. Just like that, both were staring at me. Jillian pointed at me, then the dogs, and finally, back to the boy.

The man nodded, but not before reaching for his own phone. Jillian, it would seem, must have warned him what was going to happen, and suggested he record the encounter. You want your son to experience a full, corgi introduction? Hey, I can make that happen.

"Would you like to meet them?"

The boy nodded again. I then pointed at the freshly mowed grass.

"Perhaps you should sit on the grass there."

The youngster turned to look at the lawn. He shrugged, walked over to the grass, and dropped into a cross-legged sitting position.

"Are you ready?"

The boy nodded a third time, and then looked at me as though he thought I was just another crazy adult. I squatted next to the dogs, draped an arm around each of them, and decided to up the ante. Any dog owner will know how to rile up their dogs. I was certainly no different.

"Do you want to meet him? Are you ready?"

Both dogs were wriggling so bad that you would have thought they knew the boy and hadn't seen him for months.

"All right. *Release!*"

Both corgis took off like a shot. The kid's eyes widened with surprise, but before he could say anything, two horizontal tornados reached their destination. Sherlock and Watson collided with the boy and knocked him onto his back. Then, in true corgi fashion, they plastered wet doggie kisses all over his face. I didn't know who was enjoying himself more, the giggling boy or the laughing father. I think we clearly made someone's day.

A blue 1967 Corvette Stingray pulled up and parked alongside the curb, behind the landscaper's truck. A woman in her late twenties appeared, wearing a thick green sweater and ripped blue jeans. She noticed the frolicking dogs and immediately veered toward them.

Watson, barking excitedly next to her packmate as Sherlock continued to lick the boy's exposed face, noticed the approaching woman first. My red and white corgi yipped once and tore off after her. Moments later, Sherlock zipped by me, eager to reach the woman first.

"Sherlock! Watson! Hi, guys! How are you doing today, you cute-as-a-button doggies?"

"Hi, Dottie!" Jillian said, as she arrived at my side. She checked her watch. "You're right on time."

Dottie Hanson, daughter of the late Clara Hanson, had become a new permanent fixture in our lives, it would seem. Having no other friends in

PV, and no family she could turn to, Dottie latched on to us and seemed to view Jillian and myself as her surrogate parents.

I looked at my fiancée with confusion on my face. "On time? For what? Did I forget something?"

"Always," Jillian laughed. "In this case, Dottie is here to give us her opinion on the flatware and china we selected."

"Wedding stuff," I sighed. "Of course."

"Men," Jillian giggled. "Well, come on, Dottie. I can't wait to show you what we've picked out so far. We've narrowed the china down to four different possibilities. It'll be interesting to see if you can pick out which of us selected which patterns."

"I can't wait to be of help," Dottie gushed. "And the flatware?"

"There are two choices," I told the girl. "Truth be told, I think the two of us are okay with either choice. However, it'd be nice if you picked the right one, of course."

"Oh, great, no pressure there, Zack."

I started up the front steps, intent on following the dogs and the girls inside. There, on the second step from the top, was the boy's video game. Turning, I could see father and son having an animated discussion, with the kid doing most of the talking. Plus, he was rambling on so fast that you'd think he was practicing to become an auctioneer.

Glancing down at the game as I covered the distance to the duo, I saw that I had been right. The boy had been playing a video game, and an old one at that. There were no fancy graphics, and no high-def displays. This particular game used vector graphics, and depicted a space game where you were trying to blow up enemy ships. Bad guys zipped around the screen so fast that it's a wonder someone that young could play it. There's no way I'd survive ten seconds playing that game.

That was about the time I remembered where I had seen that game before. As a matter of fact, I had played it before, and since I know you're going to ask, I'll admit it: I sucked at it. I must've lost stacks of quarters playing that game at the local arcade. I will also say that it was nice to see the younger generation interested in playing those older, 8-bit games. Remembering the dogs had stared at the device for a few moments, I decided to snap a few pictures.

Making it inside, I immediately heard the girls laughing at one of the china designs, claiming that the pattern was 'too busy' and 'wouldn't go with anything'. Yes, they could have been talking about one of Jillian's choices, but let's face it, I already knew they were talking about one of mine. The pattern in question was bold, bright, and full of colors. Personally, I thought it was a good choice. Then again, that must explain why Jillian refrained from voicing her opinion, citing her decision to wait for Dottie, instead.

Now, I could see why. Like minds think alike, I suppose. The pattern they ended up selecting was a basic white, with a gently scalloped edge and some type of metal trim around the edge of the plate. Or bowl, I guess.

"Do you see?" Jillian was saying. "This set, while basic in your eyes, is perfect."

"Exactly," Dottie agreed.

"Why?" I inquired. "It looks boring."

"Think how many different colors it can go with," Jillian insisted.

"What colors are you talking about?" I asked, trying hard to keep my exasperation out of my voice. "Am I missing something? Are you planning on mixing this set with another?"

"Show him the Christmas plates," Jillian instructed, as she looked over at Dottie. "Then, he'll see what we mean."

"Christmas plates?" I lamely repeated. "You're going to mix this set with Christmas plates? I don't see ... oh. Oh, I get it."

Yes, I finally did. Jillian was thinking long term. The Christmas plate Dottie was showing me was sitting directly on top of one of Jillian's newly selected white plates. That was why she wanted white. It was generic enough to be used with any other colored plate, be it Christmas, or Halloween, or essentially any other holiday.

"It looks great," I admitted. "Objections withdrawn. Great choice, you two."

Both girls beamed at me.

For the next four hours, the girls ... yeah, you read that right. Four hours! As I was saying, for the next four hours Jillian and Dottie perused thick, glossy magazines, consulted numerous websites, and made extensive notes in a huge, white three-ring binder. What was I doing? Well, I managed to entertain myself by playing with the dogs and, between the frenetic random activity periods, or FRAP sessions for you fellow dog owners, I went over notes for the completed draft of the special novel I had written as an homage for Vance and Tori's anniversary. By the time I looked up, the sun had long since retired, and it was pitch black outside.

"Would either of you like anything to drink?" I asked, as I stood up to stretch my legs.

"Thank you, Zachary. Dottie? Would you care for something to drink?"

"Holy cow. Is that the time? Is it really 9:30 at night?"

"It is," I confirmed, as I stretched my back.

"I had no idea it was so late. I should really be getting home."

"Same time tomorrow?" Jillian hopefully asked.

Askance, Dottie glanced over at me.

"Pretty please?" I added. I made a point of looking at all the materials laid out on the table before the two of them. "You wouldn't want to subject me to any of that, would you?"

Dottie laughed and eventually nodded. "If you're okay putting up with me, then I'd love to help."

"You're on," I said, nodding. "Just let me …"

"Oh my! We can fly! You can fly! We can fly! Come on, everybody, here we go!"

I sheepishly reached for my phone. "Sorry 'bout that. I really need to rethink that ringtone."

"That's from Disney's Peter Pan, isn't it?" Dottie asked.

I nodded. "That's right. I use it for Vance, who's a detective on the force."

"Why would you use the song from Peter Pan?" Dottie asked.

"Check YouTube," I chuckled. "Hey, Vance. What's up?"

"Zack? Good. You're still awake. Um, you are, aren't you?"

"Yeah, Jillian and Dottie were going over some wedding stuff and lost track of time. Seeing as how I don't have to do it, I wasn't about to interrupt them."

"Smart man, buddy. Listen, I know it's late, but I was wondering if I could get you and the dogs to do me a favor?"

"You want us to do you a favor? Right now? Okay, sure, I guess. What do you need, pal?"

"Get over to Gary's Grocery on the double. They received their shipment of supplies tonight, and ..."

"... they finally have cranberries? Awesome. We're on it."

"They've closed for the night, you doofus. I'm trying to tell you that, sometime after they closed, they received their shipment. Wouldn't you know it, they were hit. Do you get it? PV has been hit!"

SIX

W e were just here, earlier today," I stated, as the dogs and I strolled into the darkened store that was Gary's Grocery. I looked over at Vance and then pointed down at the dogs. "Do they have permission to come in here?"

"Are you kidding me?" Vance scoffed. "Gary was asking for you guys, personally. He's on his way in, by the way."

"If he's not here," I slowly began, hooking a thumb back at the front door, "then how did we get in? How did *you* get in, for that matter? Who unlocked the door?"

Vance pointed toward the back of the store. "His night manager is currently here, as are the two clerks who helped receive the shipment from their distributor."

I led the dogs farther into the store and automatically glanced over at the closed-off pharmacy. The security gate was in place, and didn't appear to have been tampered with. A few dozen steps took me by the liquor section, and I could clearly see that it hadn't been touched, either. Confused, I looked over at Vance and pointed at the booze.

"Pharmacy is untouched. Alcohol is still on the shelves. If this was the same criminal then that would suggest something else was meant to be the diversion. So, was there? A diversion, I mean?"

Vance nodded, and pointed back toward the front of the store and customer service counter, where cigarettes and movies were sold in a variety of formats.

"This time, it looks like it's baby formula. You'd be surprised just how much that crap costs. It's usually kept in a locked display case at the front of the store."

"Baby formula?" I scoffed. "Seriously? I don't get it. If these burglaries are being done by the same person, then they would have to be … well …"

"… the stupidest thing walking around on two legs?" Vance finished. "Agreed. I don't know who they're fooling, but it sure as hell isn't us. This makes me think we're dealing with a complete noob here."

"How'd he get in?" I asked. "Picked the lock on another door?"

"I haven't found any evidence to support that," Vance informed me, with a sigh. Then, he handed me his flashlight. "Do me a favor and do a perimeter check outside, okay? This is one piece of the puzzle that doesn't fit with the rest."

I nodded. "Will do. If this is our same guy, then he had to have picked *something* to get in here."

"His nose, his butt, I don't really care," Vance grumbled. "Call me if you find something. I have to wait here, since Gary is bound to show up sooner or later."

"Roger that. Sherlock? Watson? Come on, guys. Let's head outside."

We walked outdoors and I steered the dogs to the right. Gary's Grocery might not have been as big as a regular, full-sized grocery store, but it was definitely bigger than Vicki's Grab-n-Go and Medford's El Gato. Maybe there was a side door, or maybe even a back door, somewhere on the building that Vance missed? If so, then I was confident the dogs could find it.

As carefully as we could, we made our way around the building, navigating abandoned carts, stacks of pallets, and several large bales of compressed cardboard. The dogs sniffed a few things here and there, and hesitated only briefly at one of the cardboard bales, but had moved off by the time I got my phone out. If it had been something they truly wanted me to take a picture of, then they wouldn't have budged until I had done so.

I was about to think that there was nothing outside worth mentioning, but then the three of us rounded the northwestern corner of the building and came upon the dual loading docks. This was where the large semi-trucks would back their trailers down a short ramp so that the trailers would be at ground level and could be easily off-loaded. Running parallel to the ramp was a large, enclosed machine, complete with a metal rect-angular chute connecting it to the same wall as the loading doors. Maybe it was a garbage chute?

"Cardboard," I decided, as I noticed more of the huge bales nearby.

The dogs were staring up at the chute, as though they could hear someone moving around in it. It got me thinking. That chute? It looked big enough to admit a man. Could someone have crawled *up* that chute to gain entry to the store? If so, then they'd have to hop inside the compactor and climb up to the top of the machine, where the chute terminated. Was there anything to prevent someone from entering that chute?

"Don't move, guys," I ordered the dogs. "I want to see something."

Being careful not to touch the side, or the inter-ior, of the compactor, I leaned over and shone my flashlight up at the chute's entrance. Sure enough, there was a large, metal flap covering the mouth of the chute. However, I didn't see any latches, or any type of device which would prevent a person from simply prying the flap up and heading up the short chute and gaining access to the building. Now, don't get me wrong, it'd take one nimble-as-hell person to be able to do it. The mouth of the chute had to be four or five feet above my head inside the compactor. Granted, there were little inden-tations here and there, which would afford places one could grip, or perch, as they climbed up. So, the question was, had Vance noticed this?

"I most certainly have not," Vance replied, after I posed the question. "Good work, Zack. Have you touched anything?"

"Nope. I was careful not to touch a freakin' thing."

"Awesome. I'll send a tech over there to see about dusting for prints. Give the dogs a pat for me."

"Hey, I discovered this, not them."

"You did? Zachary, you're such a good boy! Are you a good boy? Good job, buddy!"

"Jerk," I grumbled, but not before I cracked a smile. "You owe me a beer for that."

"Deal. Keep looking around. I really want to see if the dogs notice anything else."

"You got it."

We made it around the rest of the store without any more incidents. That is, until we hit aisle nine. What was on that particular aisle? Greeting cards. Sherlock and Watson pulled me over to the cards, and they stared up at them, as if they were fascinated by their existence. Wondering whether or not they chose this particular spot for a reason, or else they picked a spot at random, I tried to lead the dogs away from the racks of cards.

Nope. Neither dog allowed themselves to be moved. Glancing up at the cards, I shrugged, and snapped a few pictures. Once done, the corgis rose to their feet and followed me around the store. I made sure to pause at the three exterior doors we encountered, just to see if either Sherlock or Watson picked up a scent or thought there was something worth investigating, but there wasn't. Neither of the dogs bothered to so much as look up.

"Anything?" Vance hopefully asked, when we met up nearly fifteen minutes later.

I shook my head. "Kinda. As of about ten minutes ago, the only thing that caught their eye was the chute at the compactor, and that's only after I pointed it out to them. I think that's our perp's point-of-entry."

"I walked back to take a look at it myself," Vance informed me. "I think you're right. I don't know if we'll be able to get any prints, but the tech *is* trying. Hey, I should tell you that Gary is finally here. He's in the back, looking through his shipment to see what's been stolen. Did you find something else?"

I presented my phone and showed Vance the pictures of the greeting cards. "Don't ask me why, but they stopped to stare at these cards. I can only assume the reason why will become clear later on."

We met up with the store owner less than ten minutes later. He might be a slender, timid man in his late sixties, but don't let that fool you. This was someone who usually avoided confrontation, but that was only when his business wasn't concerned. If you try to tell him how to run his store, then you were more than likely going to be told to go fly a kite. Gary had been working in the grocery industry since his teenage years, and knew pretty much everything there was to know about running a successful, *profitable* grocery store.

Together, Vance, the dogs, and I headed inside the store and angled for the employee-only doors leading into the back storeroom.

"No good, punk-ass juvenile delinquents," we heard a voice grumbling. "That's what's wrong with society nowadays."

"What?" I heard a much younger voice ask.

"Corporal punishment. If the threat of physical punishment was on the table, then I guaran-damn-tee you crap like this wouldn't happen."

Vance and I rounded the corner and saw Gary, huddled over his receiving desk, poring through what was presumably the shipping invoice for his latest delivery. Two teenage stock boys were lingering nearby, each with a fearful expression on their face.

"Answer me this," Gary was saying, as he skimmed through the multi-page invoice, "would either of you break into a business knowing that, should you be caught, you'd be whipped? Or caned, like they do in Singapore or Malaysia?"

Both kids vehemently shook their heads no.

"It needs to happen here," Gary muttered, as he irritably flipped the page of his invoice.

Vance cleared his throat. Gary looked up at us. I could see one very exasperated store owner glare at us for a few moments before his eyes dropped to stare at the dogs. Just like that, his shipping invoice was forgotten and he knelt down on the ground, bringing him down to the dogs' level. Both Sherlock and Watson knew this, which was why they switched to their Clydesdale personas and physically yanked me over to Gary's side.

"Sherlock and Watson! Oh, you brighten my day, guys. Tell me you'll make an old man happy and say that you've found something?"

With this, Gary looked hopefully up at me. I ended up shrugging.

"We're still looking, but we do believe we've found out how the perp got in here."

"That's no surprise," Gary grumbled. He turned to point back toward the front entrance. "Did you see what those little jerks did to my front door?"

"Believe it or not, Mr. Gardner," Vance began, "we believe that was just a diversion. We've found another point of entry, and we think it's how the perp gained entry."

"Oh? Enlighten me."

"Your compactor," I answered.

"My compactor?" Gary repeated, confused. "There's no way someone could make it inside through my compactor. Sure, there's a chute leading from the building to the machine, but ... are you saying someone found a way to get inside?"

"There wasn't much to it," Vance sighed. "I don't know if you've ever looked inside that thing before, but if you did, you'd see that there's a flap inside, which is typically closed. Now, the only thing keeping that chute closed is a single spring. Get yourself a flat-head screwdriver and you'll be able to pry the flap open and, if you're small enough, you can crawl back through the chute and make it inside."

"Your theory is that the person who did this is small," Gary began, sounding skeptical, "and instead of breaking down the front door, which is currently broken, I might add, you think he snuck in through our cardboard baler. Did I hear you right?"

Vance nodded. "You did. As you are probably aware, stores were hit in Grants Pass and Medford. The MO is the same: discreet entry, a very obvious attempt at a diversion, and then—oddly enough —the theft of cranberries is discovered. How am I doing so far?"

"Cranberries," Gary breathed. "Well, I'll be a monkey's uncle."

"Your cranberries were already sold out." I reminded the store owner.

Gary tapped his shipping invoice. "I've got a buddy who works at the distribution center. He was able to get me every freakin' thing I ordered. I feel I should tell you something. In all the years I've been in this business, never once have I seen a bare shelf in one of the stores I've worked, let alone the one I have owned and operated. So, I made incredibly certain I would be able to plug those holes."

"You had more cranberries on order," I

breathed. "Tell me you have a bag or two left. Jillian needs some for a few of her recipes."

Gary turned to regard me with a neutral expression. "Jillian? As in, Jillian Cooper, owner of Cookbook Nook?"

I nodded, and held up my left hand. "That's the one. She's my fiancée."

"I would have given her a few bags, on the house," Gary sadly informed me, "seeing how she's such a good customer. If only …"

"… they wouldn't have been stolen," Vance finished, after Gary trailed off.

"Yes," Gary sighed. He straightened, and then headed for the swinging doors leading back to the store. He then pointed at the closest shelf. "These break-ins have caused the people to hoard their supplies and incited excess panic-buying. That's why the shelves are so bare. Nothing is happening to my deliveries. I still get the same amount of supplies, in the same timely fashion as I always have. However, will any of that make a difference to the dimwitted, easy-to-frighten public? Do either of you know what this particular break-in is going to do to the people of PV?"

"It's not gonna be good," I surmised.

Gary shook his head. "No, it is not. If you thought you saw people frivolously make purchases before, then you ain't seen nuthin' yet. It's gonna get so much worse before it gets better."

"Let's hope you're wrong on that count," Vance informed the business owner. "Mr. Gardner, let me ask you something. You obviously received this shipment tonight, right?"

Gary nodded. "That's right."

"And the store was closed?"

"We closed at 9 p.m. tonight," Gary confirmed. "The shipment arrived at around 10 p.m. The driver was nice enough to send me a text when he was close. That way, I could arrange for someone to be here to open the store."

"Makes sense," I murmured.

Sherlock and Watson settled to the ground and were content to watch us bipeds talk.

"How soon after the shipment was received did your alarm go off?" Vance asked. His notebook was open and he was busy taking notes.

Gary sighed. "What, you want me to say it? Fine. It's too convenient."

"What is?" I inquired. "When did the burglars hit?"

"Fifteen minutes later," Gary acknowledged.

"The perp was already in the store, wasn't he?" Vance guessed. "Or, at the very least, he was concealed outside as he was staking out the store. He —or she, I suppose—waited a quarter of an hour to make certain the coast was clear. That's when they made their move, wasn't it?"

Gary nodded. "That's it, as far as I can tell."

"So, what was stolen?" I asked. "Was it really some baby formula? I'd think there'd be many more things a burglar would want than baby formula."

"Why do you think it's kept under lock and key?" Gary countered. "Formula is a hot commodity, I'm sorry to say. Damn, thieving hooligans."

Vance snapped his fingers. "That reminds me ... Officer Jones? Are you out there? Could you come here a second?"

A tall, lean officer with hair long enough to be considered a mullet and eyebrows that looked as though two spiders had taken up residence on his face, appeared in the doorway.

"Detective? You called?"

"I need you to do something for me, pal."

"Name it, Detective."

"Take Simpson and head out. Look for nearby dumpsters, or abandoned cars, or anywhere someone would stash a large quantity of stolen merchandise. I kid you not, if the same person who perpetrated the last two robberies is responsible for this one, then he's already ditched the merchandise."

"Then, why steal it in the first place?" Officer Jones asked.

"To throw us off the scent," I supplied. "And, for the record, I'd like to point out it's not working."

"What are we looking for here?" Jones asked.

"Baby formula," Vance answered. "Instant and liquid, from the looks of thing. Canisters, cartons, bottles of liquid, if it has the word 'formula' on it, be on the lookout for it. The merchandise might be in boxes, or it might be in duffel bags. You won't know until you find it."

"If it's out there, then we'll find it," Officer Jones promised.

Once Jones had left, Vance turned to Gary and gestured at the thick shipping invoice that was still on the receiving desk.

"Was there anything else missing besides the cranberries?"

"Weirdest theft I've ever seen," Gary muttered. He motioned for one of his clerks to hand him the invoice. Once he had it, he started flipping through the pages. After a few moments, he shook his head. "Three boxes of frozen cranberries. That's it. That's all that's missing. I guess I should be thankful, because this could have been a whole lot worse. The stink of this is seeing how people are going to freak out. I can only hope that, once you apprehend whoever did this, you allow the dogs to bite them. Right on the keister."

Bemused, I glanced down at the dogs. Sensing we had been talking about them, both Sherlock and Watson had risen to a sitting position and were watching Gary like a pair of hawks. In fact, it looked as though Sherlock had nodded and was now anxious to be on the move again. However, try as we might, none of us could find anything else that sparked Sherlock and Watson's interest. We walked up and down the aisles. Nothing. We strolled by the pharmacy and then the liquor section. Both dogs kept their eyes (and noses) on the floor.

For kicks and giggles, we returned to the

back storerooms to see if there was anything we missed. And, for the record, there wasn't. But, it wasn't a total loss. It gave Vance and me some time to confer amongst ourselves.

"Seriously, pal," Vance was saying, "we need to nip this in the bud as soon as possible. Have you ever tried to go grocery shopping when the store is full of idiots stuck in a panic-buying mode?"

I was already nodding and then I was pointing straight down.

"Not only have I done that, but I did so right here. Today. Earlier, in fact. So, some cranberries are stolen and it makes everyone freak out? Where's the logic in that?"

"All I was trying to do was buy some flippin' toilet paper," Vance said, as we pushed our way through the swinging double doors and back into the main store. "You'd think the whole stinking town developed a case of the trots."

"At the same time," I added. "People are just weird."

"The public is weird," Vance clarified. "People are smart, but if you put enough of 'em together, then the collective I.Q. drops to subterranean levels."

I snorted with amusement and continued to follow Vance outside.

"I just can't figure out why only small stores are targeted," Vance complained, as we walked toward our cars. "Both Grants Pass and Medford are larger than we are, and each town has several large franchise stores, but did they get hit?"

"I have a pretty good idea I know the answer to this," I said. "I'm guessing the answer is no, they didn't. There must be some other connection."

"And what the hell is the deal with only taking cranberries?" Vance griped. "Sure, I like cranberry sauce with my turkey, just as much as the next person, but come on. All cranberries? Everywhere? What's the deal with that?"

"What about the diversions?" I continued. Hey, as long as we were taking the time to air our grievances, we might as well cover all the bases, right? "Who, in their right mind, would willingly steal all those drugs from the first store, only to dump them less than a mile away? As if they were afraid to be found with them?"

"Don't forget the booze from the second store," Vance reminded me.

"Drugs and booze, both of which were recovered. And this one? Any chance they'll find the stolen baby formula?"

"I'm really hoping they do," Vance confided, as he lowered his voice. "I know Gary is not going to want to replace it all."

"Doesn't he have insurance?" I quietly asked.

My detective friend nodded. "Yes, he does, but there's still a deductible to be considered."

I loaded the dogs into my Jeep and looked at my friend. "Tell me something. Are we dealing with the stupidest criminal to ever walk the earth?"

Vance chuckled. "I'm starting to think so. Whoever is doing this is ..." He trailed off as his cell began to ring. "Detective Samuelson. Hey, Jones-y, what's goin' on? You what? Hold on." My friend muted the call and looked at me. "They found the formula. It was apparently loaded into several of those disposable Styrofoam coolers which I'm guessing they stole from Gary's, and promptly dumped."

"In a dumpster?" I guessed.

"You guessed it. This dumpster was behind Rupert's Gas & Auto."

"Were they heading out of town?" I wondered aloud. "Rupert's is on the north side of town, as though you were heading to Grants Pass."

Vance unmuted the call. "Jones? Look, I know it's late, but see if you can locate any witnesses. I'd like to know where this person was headed, or if it's just a fluke. Thanks, pal."

Just then, before either of us could get in our vehicles, Gary came hurrying out of his store, holding something in each hand.

"Detective? Mr. Anderson? I have something for you."

"Whatcha got there, Mr. Gardner?" Vance wanted to know. Then he caught sight of the item Gary was holding. "Oh, I think you just made Zack's day. Hey, buddy, check it out."

I stepped around Vance to see for myself what the store owner was holding. Catching sight of the bag, my eyes lit up. Somehow, and I don't know how, he had found a bag of cranberries!

"Oh, I owe you a bottle of wine."

"I remember you mentioning you were in the market for some cranberries. Well, I have Todd and Jason going through the freezer, looking for anything else that might have been missing. Nothing is, mind you, but they did find several bags of cranberries in another box, as though they had been unpacked and ended up falling into the box below theirs. Whatever the reason, I wanted you to have this. And you, Detective. Cherish these. I don't think there are any more in our area."

"I appreciate it, Mr. Gardner," I said, as I turned to place the bag inside my Jeep. That's when I noticed both dogs were plastered to the windows, watching the store owner. Well, he was still holding Vance's bag. "What are you two looking at? Vance, would you take that bag? I want to see if they're watching ... no, they're still watching you, Mr. Gardner."

"I can see that," Gary admitted. "May I ask why?"

"I'd like to know, too," Vance admitted, as he placed his bag of the red berries inside his sedan. "Zack? What are they doing?"

I motioned Gary over. "Come here, would you? If it's truly you they are watching, then ... yep, it's you, Mr. Gardner. Look how they're watching you. Do you have something else on you?"

Gary reached behind his back and produced the shipping invoice. "I had this in my back pocket, if that helps."

I held out a hand. "May I?"

Gary passed the wad of papers to me. I started to walk around the circumference of my car. The corgis, I might add, were staring at me as though I had sprouted a tail. Vance approached and held out his own hand. Passing the papers to him, I stepped back, out of the way. Vance repeated the steps I had just done and watched with amazement as the dogs tracked his progress around my Jeep.

"It's the shipping invoice," Vance said, amazed. He looked down at the papers and then over at me. "Any idea why?"

I pulled out my cell. "Let's do this. Hold that up, would you?"

Vance held the invoice up and looked on as I snapped a few pictures of the shipping manifest. Once I was done, and my cell was back in my pocket, I caught sight of Vance flipping through the pages. Shrugging, Vance turned to hand Gary back his invoice when he paused, hand outstretched. Slowly, he brought the invoice up to his face and gripped it with both hands. Had he noticed something?

"What is it?" I wanted to know.

Vance tapped something on the invoice and turned excitedly to Gary. "This right here. I've seen this identifier before. At least, I think I have. What does this stand for?"

Gary leaned over Vance's shoulder and studied the small box Vance was tapping. "That? That's our distributor."

"What are you looking at?" I asked my friend.

Vance motioned me over and showed me the code he was referring to: MDC.

"Do you remember Vicki's Grab & Go and the boxes she reported stolen? Do you remember that funky code that was on each of the boxes?"

"Sure," I said, nodding.

Vance hastily pulled his notebook out from his pocket and flipped through a few pages before grinning triumphantly and holding the small book up.

"This ... this right here. 'MDC2146, MDC2147, and MDC2148'."

"Those were the identifiers on the boxes that were taken," I recalled. "Are those the same numbers here?"

Vance gave me a grin before he turned to Gary.

"Answer something for me, pal. Your distributor? MDC? Is that an acronym?"

"Medford Distribution Center," Gary supplied. "Not very original, I know."

"Do they supply all the grocery stores in this area with their products?" Vance wanted to know.

Gary shook his head. "No, MDC is just one of several small suppliers. There's three distribution centers in Bend; Medford has MDC and one other, I believe."

"And Grants Pass?" I asked.

"The same as us," Gary told us. "We're too small, so we need to have our products shipped in.

But, I will say, I'm glad we don't qualify as a 'big boy'."

"Why?" Vance curiously asked.

"Well, all the name brand stores get their supplies from Bend," Gary explained. "Obviously, they have farther to go, so they typically get their shipments once a week. As for us? Well, since MDC is so close, we can usually place another order and have it here within 24 hours."

"That's what you did for this delivery, wasn't it?" I asked.

Gary nodded. "Yep. Fat load of good it did me."

"Imagine getting your orders all the way from Bend," Vance breathed, amazed. "You'd think there'd be a closer distribution center."

Gary shook his head. "There's not, unfortunately."

"Bend is over 170 miles north from here," Vance told me. "Zack? I think I know why these three stores were targeted."

"No, we don't," I argued. "Nobody could want cranberries that badly, not when there are other stores more readily available than the offerings we have in our small towns."

Vance was already on his cell.

"This is Detective Samuelson. I need a records check of a company called 'MDC', short for Medford Distribution Center. I need to know … what's that? No, it's a supplier. It's … I'm sorry? No, it's the company who supplies our grocery store with their inventory. Yes, we're guessing they were the suppliers to the other two stores who were hit, too. Yes, I'll hold."

"What's going on?" Gary quietly asked me. "Was there something on my shipping invoice that shed some light on who was responsible for this?"

"I'm not sure," I admitted. "What I can tell you is that we think we finally know how your store, and the two who were previously hit, are linked."

"We have the same supplier," Gary softly guessed.

"That's right."

Gary looked at the two dogs, who had now settled down onto the back seat of my Jeep.

"How did they know?"

"Beats the hell out of me," I admitted.

I heard Vance's conversation start up again, but before I knew what was going on, he was thanking the person on the phone and hanging up.

"Zack, get this. MDC? You're right. They're the supplier for the other two stores as well."

"Which we figured," I said.

"Right. Now, all we gotta do is figure out what's so important about those stupid cranberries. I'm with you. I think there's something up with those berries. Someone doesn't want anyone to have any. I want to know why."

We thanked Gary and, again, headed to our cars.

"What's our next play?" I wanted to know.

"Tomorrow, I'm going to call MDC and find out

why someone wants to get their hands on every last bag of cranberries. Plus, I want to find out how many other small grocery stores MDC supplies. I also want to find out more about MDC's supplier. I mean, there's gotta be something up with that processing plant. I'm hoping we can ... what's wrong?"

"What processing plant?" I wanted to know.

"Oh, didn't I tell you? Apparently, MDC gets their cranberries from some plant in Washington. In case you're wondering, it was listed on MDC's official website."

"So, they get their cranberries from Washington State. How does that help us?"

"No clue, pal. We're going to have to wait until we can call them tomorrow."

SEVEN

The following morning, the dogs and I were in a small room to the right of my kitchen, affectionately named the breakfast nook, having a bite to eat. This small-ish room had bench seating and overlooked a bay window, which faced out onto my winery. Frankly, it was my favorite room in the house, and unless Jillian was here, this was where you'd typically find me. The caveat to that would be if I happened to be writing. Then, I'd be sequestered upstairs, in my study, which was simply one of my spare rooms.

It was early, much earlier than I would have liked, seeing how the corgis roused themselves a good hour before sunrise. Why, might you ask? Well, it didn't take a rocket scientist to figure out what they were doing. They were hungry. So, that meant that they needed to wake Yours Truly up. How did they decide to accomplish that feat? Well, for whatever reason, Sherlock and Watson decided to play a noisy game of tag, followed by a ferocious battle of keep-away, and finish the play session with several rounds of tug-of-war. All of this, mind you, just so happened to take place on my bed, with me in it. I knew exactly what the dogs were trying to do the moment the first corgi drive-by happened. They clearly wanted their breakfast and they were inviting me, in their own way, of course, to join them. Typically, they woke with me and we all had breakfast together. Not today, unfortunately. The little boogers decided to take it upon themselves to get themselves fed. I personally tried to hold out as long as I could by pretending to be asleep, but Watson took care of that for me. Once it became clear that *Operation Wake Daddy* had failed, my cute little girl took it upon herself to go undercover.

And I mean that *literally*.

Watson squirmed under the covers, nestled herself against my chest, and then ... let one go. Now, I'm hoping I don't have to go into detail with that one, because holy cow, did it have the desired effect. My little girl has been known, from time to time, to eat a little too fast, and therefore ingest some air along with her kibble. Well, the excess air had to go *somewhere*. In Watson's case, she could clear out a hotel lobby in less time than it takes to pinch your nose shut. The worst part was the fact that I felt a brief burst of warmth on my leg, right about where her rump would have been.

"Give me some warning, would you?" I demanded, as I practically leapt out of bed and fanned the covers in an attempt to remove the noxious brown clouds that were undoubtedly working their way *up*, through the bedding. "If you wanted me up that badly, then you should have just said so. Holy cow, Watson. What the heck have you been eating? You'd think your owner has never been responsible for feeding a corgi before."

Sherlock leapt on the bed, stretched out into the famous corgi 'sploot', and regarded me with a smug expression.

"Don't even think you won, sport. I got up because I wanted to, all right?"

Fast forward to the present time. I had just finished munching on my croissant and reached for a banana from the bowl of fruit I keep on the table in here. Just like that, I felt two pairs of canine eyes boring into the back of my skull. Grinning at my two dogs, I peeled the banana and offered each of them a small piece of the fruit. I don't know about your dogs, but mine? They love bananas so much that they've learned to recognize the sound of a single banana being broken off from a cluster.

Wandering into the living room, I turned on a local news channel and sank down into my favorite recliner to read through the local paper. However, right about that time, my cell started to ring. Glancing at the display had me automatically looking through the front window, to see if he was lurking on my front doorstep.

It was Caden, and thankfully, no, he wasn't waiting to ambush me outside my front door.

There'd be no nasty taste tests for me first thing this morning, thank you very much. What did all of that mean for me? Easy. It was safe to take the call.

"Hey, Caden. How's it goin'?"

"Zack, ol' buddy, ol' pal! How are you doing this fine, lovely day?"

Every alarm I had just went off. This was worse than putting in an appearance on my front porch. He was schmoozing me, which meant he wanted me to buy something. I could only hope it didn't have a comma in the price tag.

"Who is it for, and how much does it cost?" I automatically asked, and because I knew it'd make my winemaster laugh, I threw in a very loud sigh.

"Oh, hear me out, would you?" Caden said. "Besides, somehow I think you'll be on board this time."

"Willingly?" I asked.

"Willingly," Caden confirmed.

"Fine. Hit me with your best shot."

"As you know, it's harvest time," Caden began. "I think I told you that this will be our largest harvest to date, right?"

Forgetting that Caden couldn't see me, I nodded. "That's right. What about it?"

"Well, our storage boxes are all full."

This got my attention. We were out of room? Those storage boxes were full? I may not have been paying full attention to Caden as he explained the size of a standard storage box, which was 48" x 40" x 31", but I was certain that I remembered his claims that we had plenty for this harvest. Each container, I had been told, would accommodate somewhere around 100 lbs. of the harvested grapes. How had my master vintner been off on his estimates? My poor brain stumbled at the math involved. Uncertain how my silence should be interpreted, Caden continued on.

"I've even showed the workers how to pack around 125 pounds in the boxes, with a few approaching 150. You don't want to go over 150 pounds for any container."

"Uh, sure. How do I fit into all of this?"

"We need more containers, and I think we're going to need more storage vats. I'm not sure where I screwed up with my estimates, but I clearly didn't carry a number somewhere on my equations."

"Sure, whatever you need," I decided. "If the winery needs it, then go ahead and order it."

"Awesome. Thanks, Zack."

Assuming this was the end of the call, I started to move my phone away from my face when I noticed that the call was still connected. Curious, the phone was returned to my ear.

"Is there something else?"

"I, uh, yeah, there's something else."

Yep, there they go. Once more, my red flags started popping up, one after the other. He was reluctant to tell me something, so it had to be bad news, didn't it?

"Out with it, amigo. What's up?"

"I know how much you like to avoid the winery, whenever I hold classes, that is."

"No worries. If you need me to be scarce for a bit, then it won't be a problem. I can head over to Jillian's for the day. Plus, I really do need to get with Vance over this latest case of ours."

"That's good to hear. The number of students around here is about to increase for the next couple of weeks, and I don't want them to get in your way."

"Oh? How many are we talking about?"

"The last time I looked, nearly 30 had signed up, and for the first time ever, I had to put a cap on the total number of students: 35. Zack, I think I'm gonna hit that number."

"Is that a good thing?" I wanted to know.

"It shows you how many families are schooling their kids in the fine art of making wine," Caden proudly informed me. "Plus, the students get legitimate, hands-on experience here, at Lentari Cellars. You can't beat that anywhere."

"That sounded like a jab at Professor What's-his-face."

Professor Ferris, current head of the Oenology Department at the community college, in Medford, was Caden's old boss after he had left his position at the winery. Who knew? Anyway, Caden had bailed on the winery when there was a better than average chance Abigail Lawson would be able to wrest control of the business away from her mother. Thankfully, she was unsuccessful, and the winery passed to me. I tracked down Caden, offered him his old job back and the rest, as they say, is history. But, with Caden Burne back at the helm, we've been flourishing.

Expanded acreage, added equipment to make day-to-day operations easier, and having full control over all decisions, Caden was having the time of his life. Additionally, even though he made plenty of money at his regular job, he still taught at the college; however, the classes he taught were all held here at Lentari Cellars. Having met Professor Grump only the one time, I can only imagine Caden kept his part-time teaching gig just to annoy Professor Ferris. After all, Caden received much higher ratings from the students than did the Grouch, and the aforementioned Grouch was supremely ticked off at having one of his underlings be more favored than he was.

Pompous jerk.

"Did I tell you he's retiring?" Caden cut in.

This was news to me.

"No, you didn't. That's great, right? Let the old sourpuss return to whatever rock he crawled out from."

"It's good, yeah, but the college wants me to take on his classes."

"I realize I don't have any set hours for you," I cautiously began, "but every time I see you, you always seem to have a million things on your plate. Are you going to have time to do that?"

"Not a chance," Caden laughed. "I told them thanks, but no thanks. My life is full enough."

"Good. Glad to hear it, amigo."

"Thanks for the support, Zack. I'll get those containers ordered."

"Send me the bill."

"I always do."

Setting my phone down, I glanced over at the dogs. Both had jumped up onto my recliner and settled on either side of me. Sherlock turned to regard me for a few moments.

"He thinks I'm a walking ATM," I tried to explain.

Sherlock snorted, and was about to return to his nap, when he glanced over at the television. I may have had the volume muted, but the channel was still on, which was currently tuned to one of those 24-hour news channels. This particular one was showing me headlines for the past twenty minutes. Disinterested, I returned to my paper.

Watson chose that time to wake up and change positions on my lap. She snuggled up against my chest and, while I was stroking her fur with my left hand, settled back down. At this time, the news program switched stories, and was now talking about some type of space program, I think.

I returned to the comics section. Laughing through the antics of an orange and black-colored tabby cat, I felt Sherlock shift positions next. Glancing over at him, I could see that he was now laying, Sphinx-like, on my right leg.

"Could your Royal Canineships stop fidgeting? It's very distracting. May I offer a pillow?"

I was ignored. Whatever. My eyes returned to my paper, but not before I glanced up at the TV. The story was still about space. It was probably to let us know of some impending eclipse, or possibly the arrival of a meteor shower.

I still wasn't paying too much attention to the television. And, if you haven't figured it out yet, I really should have. But, even though I had lost my attention, I was about to get it back.

The picture on the television shifted to an interview, and as a result, the screen brightened considerably, which is what caused me to look up again. Now, I feel I should tell you my TV was currently set to display closed captions whenever the mute button was pressed. Since I had automatically muted the TV when Caden called, the scrolling captions had instantly appeared. As I sat there, feeling both of my legs going numb thanks to the dead weight of the dogs, I started skimming through the scrolling text.

I still wasn't paying too much attention.

The video shifted again. This time, I was looking at a 15" refracting telescope, housed in a building that had been constructed in 1895. The captions mentioned something about celestial views and wonders of the universe.

Having had an interest in astronomy for quite some time now, I was now watching the program, but I still wasn't paying too close attention. The scene shifted to an exterior shot once more, which was back on the reporter standing outside the observatory's front entrance. The guy was yammering again, and I'm sorry to say, I was about to lose interest when Sherlock fidgeted, but this time, the little snot stepped on the remote, which had the unfortunate effect of unmuting the program and cranking the volume up to a level hitherto only found in rock-n-roll concerts.

Watson and I nearly jumped out of our skins. Sherlock, the smug little booger, stepped off the volume and settled back in the (now vacant) recliner. Snatching the remote and hammering away at the volume down button, I glared at Sherlock's smug visage when I heard the words 'University of Washington' come out of the reporter's mouth.

Suddenly, I was paying attention. This observatory was part of the University of Washington? They were located, unsurprisingly enough, in Washington State, which is our northern neighbor. Didn't Vance tell me the processing plant he was going to research was somewhere in the Evergreen State? What were the chances that a news story associated with Washington State would appear on television today? And not to mention, both corgis had been watching it? Was that a coincidence?

At that exact moment, in the background, a semi-truck hauling an open trailer, drove by. The diesel engine was loud, and the reporter had to pause as the truck passed, but I didn't care about any of that. Both dogs had perked up, and I'm ashamed to say, so had I, as though the three of us had suddenly heard a strange noise. Together, Sherlock, Watson, and I stared at the truck as it drove past, on the video. Why?

The truck was hauling a huge load of cranberries.

Apparently, my luck ran out. The report about the observatory was over, and the news program moved to its next story. As for me, however, I was *sprinting* for my laptop. A news story just happens to be on television, with both dogs watching? And Sherlock unmutes the channel and scares ten years of life off me to get my attention? Well, I might've lost my attention for the past fifteen minutes, but I certainly had it back now.

There it was. A quick search for cranberry processing plants in Washington State only yielded one, and it was near the University of Washington campus. That was clearly the right one. This *had* to be the plant supplying MDC with its berries. After all, there were no other candidates in the entire state. Best to be sure, though.

I expanded my search and discovered the answer: yes. That one plant processed every berry harvested in Washington and Oregon. Therefore, it had to be connected. Why would Sherlock want me to notice it? I mean, a simple internet search would have yielded the same results, and I'm positive I would have done that exact search the following day. Why now?

I thought back to the observatory and the reporter. What was the, er, story there? Obviously, the processing plant was next door to the University of Washington's campus, so could the two events have been related? Had something happened that would tie the two facilities together?

Let me pause here, for a moment, to gloat. Yes, I know it's not very becoming, but it's not often that Yours Truly stumbles across the key to cracking the current case we were working on *wide open*. As luck would have it, this particular observatory, the only one available for the University of Washington's students, had been studying the asteroid belt. It's also when I learned about ET.

No, it's not what you think. Allow me to elucidate.

The asteroid belt is a torus-shaped band of an inordinate amount of solid objects, varying in size from grains of rice all the way up to something called 'minor planets'. For the record, this huge collection of objects is located between Jupiter and Mars, and in case I've inadvertently freaked you out, the combined mass of all the varying sizes of asteroids is only about 3% of our moon.

See? Not so bad. But, I digress. The reason I mention this is to establish context.

A group of students had been studying one of the largest asteroids in the belt, which, believe it or not, had a name: Ceres. Now, every so often, as any astronomer will tell you, asteroids will come into contact with other asteroids, and the resulting collisions will oftentimes knock them out of their trajectory, much like one croquet ball striking another. Some of those asteroids are then capable of reaching the Earth. On an average day, there are usually about 17 meteors which earn the right to upgrade themselves to 'meteorite', meaning they manage to strike the surface of the Earth. Water, land, it didn't matter. Thankfully, most burn completely up before they make contact, which means the resulting meteorite is typically the size of a pebble, and no larger than a fist. That may sound like a lot, but when there's an estimated 25 million objects entering our atmosphere on a daily basis, ranging in size from a grain of rice to the size of a car, and of those, fewer than two dozen manage to make it all the way down, there really is no need to panic.

Now, let's take a moment and talk about those select few which are large enough, or durable enough, to withstand entry and make contact with the Earth. One such meteor strike resulted in a leftover specimen that weighed nearly ten pounds. Buried inside was something that most people would never expect to find inside a meteorite, and that was a diamond.

Diamonds in meteors are not as uncommon as you may think. Some scientists believe that diamonds are found within stars and may very well be one of the first minerals ever created. However, most specimens are on the microscopic side, being no more than a couple of nanometers long.

Somehow, and it wasn't revealed how, this particular meteorite contained an extraterrestrial diamond that weighed in at 10 carats. To say it was remarkable, and extremely rare, would be an understatement. Then, much to the school's horror, some as-yet-unnamed member of the faculty took 'ET', as it was being called, to a fellow staff-member, who happened to be an amateur lapidarist, and according to the news report, had given it an 'old mine' cut, whatever that was. ET's final size? A very respectable 9 carats.

That was what had been stolen at the observatory. Someone had walked off with ET! How that ties in with Pomme Valley, I really don't know. Not yet, anyway. But, this was something Vance needed to know about.

I looked down at Sherlock and saw that he was watching me with a smug expression on his face. Sighing, I retrieved the box of doggie biscuits I kept in the kitchen and handed several to each corgi.

"Here. Vance will give me hell if I don't do this. Good job, guys. I'm pretty sure you've identified the motivation behind these robberies. Now we need to let him know what we've found. Want to go for a ride?"

Thirty minutes later, the dogs and I were strolling through the Pomme Valley police department. I say strolling, 'cause I've been here numerous times now and I am fairly well known. However, after being stopped for the fifth time, so the corgis could be greeted, I will reluctantly amend that statement to say, Sherlock and Watson were very well known. So well, in fact, that they were considered celebrities. I honestly think that it might have something to do with the simple fact those two dogs have solved more cases than the entire PV police force combined.

And before you ask, no, it's not something I typically bring up.

Walking past the information desk, where Julie, my friend Harry's wife, was sitting, we headed down the hall, toward the heart of the station. It was where all the officers had their desks, Captain Nelson had his office, and Vance had his tiny office. Through *that* doorway there was the large holding cell, and through *that* big, heavy door were the cells. The station also had a basement, where off-duty officers could make use of a small gym.

The farther we walked into the station, the more amazed I became. Was it any wonder? My first visit to this particular building wasn't a pleasant one. And now? Every single person we passed, whether they were an officer or a simple clerk, stopped to give the dogs a pat on the head, or a scratch behind the ear. As for me? I got a smile and a nod.

Oh, well.

Sherlock and Watson wove around the many

people standing about and were on a direct course to Vance's office. Visible through the door, my friend was on the phone and was pacing around the tiny confines of his office. He saw the three of us and immediately returned to his desk, sat down, and pulled out a box of doggie biscuits from one of the drawers. Vance held up two biscuits, which resulted in me getting physically dragged over to the small office. Letting go of the leashes, I watched both corgis circle Vance's desk, timidly approach, and automatically drop into a sitting position.

Those little boogers never behaved like that for me, I can tell you. All that was needed to make this a picture-perfect Kodak moment was the appearance of two halos, over Sherlock and Watson's heads. Brown-nosers.

While Vance continued his conversation on his phone, I felt a tap on my shoulder. Turning, I saw Captain Nelson standing behind me. His mouth opened, and was about to ask a question, when he noticed two leashes trailing behind Vance's desk. The captain's face lit up as his eyes landed on the two dogs, who had both turned at the appearance of Vance's boss.

"Mr. Anderson? Are you here about the grocery store break-ins?"

I nodded and stepped outside Vance's office. "Yep. There are three that I'm aware of: Grants Pass, Medford, and unfortunately, PV. Are you looking for an update?"

"Have there been some new developments?" the captain wanted to know.

I shrugged. "For all I know, Vance might already be aware of this, but I was watching the news this morning and saw something that might explain what the perp is after."

"We already know," the captain told me, using a quiet tone. He had noticed Vance was now gesturing at something behind his desk, and saw that he was in the midst of a phone call.

The captain knew about ET? Rats. Deflated, I sighed.

"I don't suppose you could tell me *why*," Captain Nelson continued.

"Er, why *what*?" I asked.

"Why would this perp want to steal cranberries? I've been a police captain for over 20 years, but this is a new one on me. This case? It just doesn't make any sense."

Ah! He didn't know after all. Captain Nelson, who had been studying my face, saw that I had something to add, and promptly leaned against the closest wall. He motioned for me to continue. However, before I could, Vance finished his call and strode out his office.

"Zack! What ... Captain Nelson? I didn't see you there. Can I do something for you, sir?"

"Make any progress with MDC?" the captain asked. I watched Captain Nelson throw me a sidelong look, which told me he wasn't about to let the matter with me drop. "What did they say about the three stores that were hit?"

Vance held up his notebook. "I've got a complete list of everyone they've done business with in the area. Granted, it's not much of a list, but there are five other stores we didn't know about. I'm going to put in calls to each of them to see if there's been any unusual activity."

"Good. Mr. Anderson? Is there something you'd like to add to the discussion?"

Vance suddenly focused his attention on me. "Zack? Why are you here? Do you have something for me?"

I shrugged. "Possibly. I have a theory. Well, *they* have a working theory," I amended as I pointed down at the dogs, "about what might be going on. I think I may have an idea about what our perp might be looking for."

This got both the captain and Vance's attention. Vance gave the dogs a brief glance before looking back at me.

"I'm all ears. Whatcha got, buddy?"

"What do you know about the Jacobsen Observatory?"

Vance blinked a few times as he stared at me. "The *what*?"

"It's the second-oldest structure on the University of Washington's campus," Captain Nelson answered. "It's for their astronomy students. There's a large, automated telescope in there, if memory serves. What about it?"

"How do you know so much about it, sir?"

Vance curiously asked.

"U-Dub alumni, Class of '76. Go Huskies."

"Anyway," I continued, as I grinned at the captain, "there was a blurb about the observatory on the news this morning."

Captain Nelson perked up. "Oh? What about it?"

"I didn't catch all of the report," I admitted, "but I did look it up online after it was over. Turns out there's been a theft."

It was Vance's turn to look interested. "At an observatory? What was stolen?"

"ET."

Vance cocked his head. "Huh?"

"What was that?" Captain Nelson asked, at the same time.

"ET," I repeated, as I grinned at my friend.

"Ha ha, Zack," Vance groaned. "Couldn't you have come up with a better ..."

"Hear me out," I interrupted. "I'm not talking about Steven Spielberg's 1981 movie. ET is the name the astronomy department gave to an extraterrestrial diamond."

"What the hell is an extraterrestrial diamond?" Vance scoffed.

Captain Nelson stared at me for a few moments before he shrugged. "Meteors."

I nodded. "You got it. I guess it's not unheard of to find diamonds in meteorites, only they're usually super small. This one, though, was 9 carats. That's what was stolen."

"When?" Captain Nelson wanted to know.

"The article I pulled up didn't say," I confessed. "I tried to find out more about it, but couldn't find anything. Maybe the university is trying to keep that piece of info out of the media?"

Captain Nelson strode over to the closest desk, which happened to be Vance's, and reached for the phone.

"I'll find out with one phone call. Give me a sec. Let's see if I still remember the number. Hello? Professor Roger Newman, please. Yes, I'll hold." The captain looked over at us. "Newman was in my graduating class, and he … Roger? It's Dale Nelson, down in Pomme Valley. I … yes, *that* Dale. How're you doing, buddy? Listen, we saw reports of a theft at Jacobsen earlier today. They're saying something about a fancy diamond being stolen. Is there any truth to that? There is? Can I ask what's so special about this diamond? Uh huh. Gotcha. Okay, thanks, partner. I appreciate it. Yes, we should catch up. I'll call you this weekend. Thanks, Roger."

"There *was* a theft," I said, as I looked at Vance.

"Mr. Anderson was correct," Captain Nelson stated, as he straightened and rejoined us outside Vance's office. "We're talking about a priceless scientific discovery which cannot be replaced. Not to mention the fact that this ET thing? It's a large diamond. Apparently, it posed too tempting of a target for someone there at the observatory."

"Do we know who?" Vance asked. "Do they have

any suspects?"

Captain Nelson shook his head. "Roger didn't say. The only thing he could confirm was the theft, which they had tried to keep quiet, only their luck finally ran out."

"Why?" I asked. "If they're looking for some-one, then wouldn't it be more prudent to alert the media and, therefore, get this perp's information out in the open?"

"You'd think, and I would think," Vance re-torted. "Listen, why don't we ..."

"There's something else you need to hear," I quickly interrupted. "It's the reason the dogs and I came down here."

"Was it on the news?" Captain Nelson asked.

"Well, yes and no," I answered, as I shrugged. "It wasn't specifically mentioned, but it was what I saw in the background: a semi-truck."

"What about it?" Vance wanted to know.

"It was hauling a load of cranberries," I smugly reported. "It was headed to a big processing plant *right next door* to the observatory."

Captain Nelson looked straight at Vance and pointed at his office. "Back on the phone. Call MDC. Find out if the cranberries that were stolen were supplied by that processing plant."

Vance nodded. "I'm on it."

"Good work, Mr. Anderson," the captain praised.

"I'd really like to take the credit, but it wasn't me."

"It was the dogs, wasn't it?" Captain Nelson asked, as he grinned down at the corgis.

"Yep. I had the TV muted, and Sherlock unmuted it, just in time for me to hear the tail end of the news story. Then, as I was watching it, I noticed the truck in the background."

The captain squatted next to the corgis, which had the unfortunate effect of both of his knees cracking so loudly that I thought he had stepped on some bubble-wrap. He looked up at me, smiled sheepishly, and returned his attention to the dogs. After a few moments, he straightened.

"Sooner or later, I'm gonna do that and not be able to make it back up."

"Please," I scoffed. "I'm already there."

The captain laughed, just as Vance exited his office. He was nodding and grinning like a kid at Christmas.

"You called it, sir. That plant handles everything in Washington and Oregon."

"That's how they smuggled the diamond out of the observatory," Captain Nelson guessed. "I'm thinking whoever the perp is, he slipped next door and stashed the stone in one of the bags of cranberries."

"That's why the stores were hit," Vance confirmed. "The perp was looking for the bag which has his diamond in it."

"The university's diamond," the captain corrected.

"Right. Plus, get this, MDC confirmed three

more clients of theirs had been burglarized."

"Where?" the captain wanted to know.

"Gold Beach, Port Orford, and Klamath Falls."

"All in the southern part of the state," the captain quietly mused.

"How long ago?" I asked.

The captain turned to Vance, who immediately pulled out his notebook. "Late last week."

"Over how many days?" I curiously asked.

Vance scratched the side of his head. "Does it matter, Zack?"

I shrugged. "Kinda. I thought it might be relevant."

"Well, let's see. Looks like it happened over the weekend. Two happened Saturday night, while the third was Sunday night."

"So, those three were the first stores to be hit?" Captain Nelson asked.

"Yes," Vance confirmed. "Does that help us?"

"Why weren't they reported?" Captain Nelson demanded.

"The only thing MDC could tell me was each of the stores had minimal damage and only a box or two of the cranberries were stolen."

"And, yet, the perp tried to make it appear as if someone else robbed the next three stores," I recalled. "I wonder why?"

"It's like they were deliberately trying to pin the blame on someone else," Vance decided.

Captain Nelson snapped his fingers. "Oh. Oh, that's good. So, *that* is what they were doing? Very clever. Very clever, indeed."

Vance and I helplessly looked at each other.

"Umm, could you explain that, sir?" my detective friend hesitantly asked.

"This perp," Captain Nelson began, "clearly thought the diamond would be at one of the first three stores that were targeted. When it became apparent it wasn't, and he knew he'd have to keep searching other stores, he tried to deflect the attention off of himself. How? By making it look as though something besides cranberries were being taken. He didn't want to draw any more attention to the cranberries. The last thing he would want was a spree of panic-buying."

"Which already happened," I said.

"True," Captain Nelson admitted. "Whoever this guy is, he's smart enough to know he had to act fast. The longer he waited, the more chances there'd be that Joe Q. Public would buy the exact bag he was looking for."

"Six burglaries," I breathed. I squatted next to the dogs and was rewarded with my own knees cracking. "I wonder where the seventh will be? Who else is there?"

"It's been a couple of days," Vance said, as he glanced over at a wall calendar above one of the cubicle desks. "We haven't heard of any other break-ins since ours."

"Meaning what, exactly?" Captain Nelson asked. "I'm not gonna like the answer, am I?"

Vance shook his head. "I can think of two possibilities. First, he might have just given up."

"Unlikely," I said. "He's gone to so much effort to try and find that diamond that I doubt very much he'd simply throw in the towel now."

Captain Nelson nodded. "Agreed. We're going to ignore that suggestion and move to your second."

"The second option," Vance continued, "is, if there are no more robberies, then that would mean that the perp has found what he's looking for--the diamond. He must've found it in PV!"

EIGHT

Y ou're kidding. You want to go out there and traipse along the countryside, while looking for the *one*? I mean, I don't know if you've noticed, but there's snow on the ground out there!"

"I know. Isn't it perfect?"

All right, it's time for some context. Since Vance was going to spend the day researching MDC, the plant which supplied the cranberries, and review the facts on all six burglaries in this case so far, my skills were not needed. Or, more specifically, Sherlock and Watson's. What did that mean for us? Well, we now had a day off. How were we spending it? My lovely fiancée took care of making the plans, and what she came up with absolutely floored me. She programmed my Jeep's navigational system, told me to dress warmly, and announced we were going on a road trip. I should have known something was up, because typically whenever we take a road trip, we use her SUV and not my gas-guzzling, off-roading Jeep.

Sherlock and Watson were even invited to go, which meant that, wherever we went, one of us were going to have to be with them at all times, since neither of us would dream about leaving the dogs in the car, alone, this time of year. It was simply too cold outside. Sure, the daytime was nice, but mornings and nights were downright chilly.

Where were we going? Turns out we were going to do some shopping. For what? Well, it turns out we were in the market for a tree. Before you ask, yes, we're looking for a Christmas tree.

I remember pointing at the closest calendar and mentioning it wasn't even Thanksgiving yet. After all, who would want to decorate for Christmas before we had even celebrated Turkey Day? As it turns out, quite a few people enjoy putting up a tree the month before Christmas. High on that list would be one Jillian Cooper.

I've helped her set up her decorations before, but usually those particular boxes wouldn't see the light of day until after I had eaten my weight in turkey. But, for whatever reason, this particular year has inspired Jillian to pull out all the stops. Just this morning, when the dogs and I stopped by Cookbook Nook, armed with her favorite chai drink and my bucket of soda, I found her busy pulling out boxes from a storage closet I hadn't even known existed.

I learned something about Jillian that day. If my fiancée was busy working on decorations for someplace other than her home, in this case, her business, then the chances were extremely high it would get her thinking about what decorations she'd like to see at her aforementioned home. I hadn't taken more than three or four boxes to the front counter when Jillian suddenly looked at me with a twinkle in her eye and announced she needed help with a new project. Little did I know that would mean we would be going on a day trip to a farm located 40 miles north of Medford, up in the hills.

Hours later, I didn't realize how high we were until I started seeing snow piled up along either side of the road, which was unpaved, by the way. And the road? It twisted and turned, and had hairpin turns so tight that you couldn't go faster than 10 mph or else you'd run off the edge. I should also mention that I have never been car sick in my life. Ever. However, with all the swaying of the car, from left, to right, back left, hard right, for the first time *ever*, I found myself getting queasy.

"Are you all right?" Jillian asked, as she watched me roll the window down and take a couple of gulps of cool, crisp air. "Feeling nauseous?"

"Just a little," I admitted. "I'm trying as hard as I can to keep from tasting my breakfast again. I don't think I've ever felt this unsettled in a car. I've tried so hard to ignore it."

"Well, getting out and stretching your legs will be good. You're in luck. We're here."

Directly in front of us was a large, metal arch.

Stretching from one end of the sign to the other were the words, Manson Family Christmas Tree Farm. With skepticism written all over my face, I turned to Jillian and pointed at the sign.

"Manson Family? We're at the Manson Family Farm? Seriously?"

"My family and I have purchased our trees from the Mansons every year since I can remember," Jillian protested. "They have the best trees, and we get to support a local, small business. You're okay with that, aren't you?"

"If I get shot and killed up here, then I'm coming back as a ghost to haunt you," I chuckled.

Thirty minutes later, Jillian and I were trekking through the open countryside, inspecting a variety of fir trees: Douglas, grand, noble, red, and Fraser. Jillian, I was surprised to learn, took the selection of her Christmas tree very seriously. After all, she wasn't about to pick the first one she encountered. Absolutely not. I mean, I couldn't possibly be that lucky, could I? Oh, no. Serious thought had to go into this decision. This one had an open spot on the back, while that one had branches that were curving in the wrong direction. And the one I thought would be perfect? Not conical enough.

I should also mention I was doing my absolute damnedest not to laugh at poor Sherlock and Watson. Why? Well, Jillian must've had this little excursion planned out well in advance, because the corgis were wearing little booties so their feet would be protected in the snow. They were a gift from my fiancée.

Now, if you've never seen a dog wearing booties before, prepare yourself for some gut-wrenching laughter, and we're talking pain-in-your-side, can't-breathe hilarity. Because the corgis had such short legs, whenever the booties were pulled onto their feet, their new footwear unintentionally covered their knees. What ended up happening?

The dogs couldn't bend their front legs.

Both Sherlock and Watson now appeared to be goose-stepping their way across the snow and ice. If you're not familiar with the term, think of it as a special marching step performed in ceremonial military parades. The goose step is most often associated with Nazi Germany, but its use in militaries has been fairly widespread since the late 19th century. Take that high-stepping march and imagine a short-legged dog performing it, and I can guarantee you'll end up snotting whatever drink you may be enjoying.

"I didn't think they'd look like that," Jillian was saying, as she dabbed a tissue at the corner of her eyes. "Those poor dogs."

"It keeps their feet protected," I pointed out. "You don't want them walking over the snow and ice without something to protect them. Their pads could get cut up. With that being said, I haven't laughed this hard in a while, so thanks for that!"

"I feel horrible," Jillian confessed.

"But you're laughing," I pointed out.

"Hush, Zachary."

The weather was crisp, the outside temperature was a balmy 40°F, and as I had previously pointed out, a thin layer of snow was on the ground. Plus, seeing how the dogs rarely got to encounter snow, I enjoyed watching how each of the dogs interacted with the foreign white material. Sherlock had promptly shoved his snout deep into the closest pile, as if he was an ostrich with his head in the sand. When the tri-colored corgi emerged, he had flecks of snow all across his snout and face.

Watson had taken a tentative step on the fresh snow and, unfortunately for her, managed to find a section of powder. She promptly sank several inches down, resulting in her belly dragging along the ground. She simply looked at me with an imploring look and waited for Daddy to come to her rescue, which I did. Gently lifting my little girl out of the fresh snow, I moved her back to the path we had been following, which had a firm, packed surface.

"If you don't want to get snow on your belly," I told the corgi, "then you'd best stay over here, with us."

Watson shook herself, sniffed again at the snow, and then happily followed me and Jillian deeper into the hills.

"All we gotta do is find the right tree and then

let them know which one?" I skeptically asked.

Jillian held up a red pouch. "Yes. Once we find the right tree, then I'll wrap this flag around the trunk. That will let the staff know a tree has been selected. They'll cut it down and package it up for us."

"Are there cameras out here?" I asked, as I looked around. "How are they supposed to find it? There are trees everywhere."

"There's a tiny GPS chip sewn into the flag," Jillian explained. "Trust me, they've thought of everything."

"Tell me something," I said, after another ten minutes had passed, without us finding *the* tree, I might add, "does your family typically decorate before Thanksgiving?"

Jillian shrugged. "Our family usually put the tree up the weekend after Thanksgiving."

"But, it's not even December," I protested.

"When did your family put your tree up?" Jillian wanted to know.

"I don't know. I guess it'd be the first or second week of December."

"That's not nearly enough time to enjoy the decorations," Jillian said, in mock horror. "Aside from the tree, did you put up many decorations?"

"Yeah, I guess so. Stockings, some candles, and a few wreaths. Oh! My dad always put this little contraption on the coffee table where, once you light the candles, it spins the top of it around, like ... like ... a top, I suppose."

"Did it have a couple of brass bells, so that when it spun, little angels were striking the bell?"

I snapped my fingers and looked at her with amazement. "Yes! Exactly! Did you guys have one of them, too?"

"Swedish angel chimes."

"Hmm?"

"That's what it was called: Swedish angel chimes. It was very popular. Still is, I believe."

"We gotta get one," I decided.

"Consider it done," Jillian said, giving me a warm smile. "Does your family have any other traditions you'd like to uphold?"

"Hmm. Can I get back to you on that? I'll have to think about that one."

"Of course."

"What about you?" I countered. "What did your family like to do?"

Jillian paused at the base of a 15' noble fir and carefully scrutinized it. After a few moments, she shook her head and moved off.

"My brother and I would always watch *How the Grinch Stole Christmas* on Christmas Eve. Then, we'd get to open a few presents, but only the ones from aunts, uncles, or grandparents. We'd then sing some carols while Joshua played the piano."

"I didn't know Josh played the piano."

Jillian let out an uncharacteristic sigh. "Joshua is the type of person who could pick up any instrument he wanted and begin playing it in less than ten minutes. Ever since he learned how to play the French horn, he's mastered the ability to sight read music."

"I'm picking up a wee bit of bitterness there," I joked.

Jillian smiled and swatted my arm. "Everything always came so easy to him. I guess I *am* a little jealous."

"One of these days, I'm sure I'll meet him," I vowed.

"Oh, you will. He talks about you all the time."

This brought me up short. "He does?"

"Sure! He knows you're a famous author, and has started calling you his brother-in-law, the writer."

"Does he, uh, know what *kind* of books I write?"

"Of course. That's how he learned about what you do. He was dating a girl who was a big fan of yours."

"Seriously, how do people keep figuring out who Chastity Wadsworth really is?" I demanded. "I clearly suck at keeping secrets."

Jillian laughed again and then stopped short. She pointed at a nearby tree and clapped excitedly. "That's it! That's the one! Oh, Zachary, isn't it beautiful?"

We were standing at the base of a 15' noble fir. It had a diameter (at its thickest point) of about seven feet, had slightly twisted, upcurved shoots, and tapered to a narrow, conical point. I will admit, it was a gorgeous tree.

"Umm, that one looks huge. Where are you

gonna put something that big?" I wanted to know.

"My living room, where else? It has vaulted ceilings, and I happen to know that, at its apex, there's nearly twenty feet of space in there. Here, would you do the honors?"

I took the red pouch, unzipped it, and pulled out a glorified cable tie. Wrapping it around the trunk, I caught sight of a clear, plastic tab on the opposite side of the cable tie's head, and pulled it out. Just like that, a tiny red light started flashing.

"I think we're good to go."

"Excellent. I think we're done here. Zachary, let me ask you something."

"Fire away, my dear."

"This diamond that you say was stolen from the University of Washington? Do you think the person who stole it was a professional?"

I didn't have to think about the answer. "Nope. There's nothing this person has done which has made me think the heist was pulled off by a pro."

"Are you sure? What makes you say that?"

I started ticking points off on my fingers. "Well, first, the perp is an amateur when it comes to picking a lock. Vance said he, or she, left scratches all over the thing, which is a sure sign it was picked by an amateur. Second, they tried to throw us off their trail by pretending they were interested in something else in the store, like booze, or drugs, or baby formula, and then proceeded to exit the store from the front door. And finally, the stolen loot was dumped, usually at a nearby dumpster, indicating it was never a target at all."

"Maybe they had a change of heart?" Jillian suggested.

"For all three? No, I doubt it. Plus, they chose a dump site which was less than a mile from the burglarized store. Either pack the stolen merchandise with you, or dispose of it in another town."

"What about the actual heist itself?" Jillian wanted to know. "Do we know how the diamond was stolen in the first place? By that, I mean, was the diamond in a vault? Were there guards nearby?"

"Oh, I get it. You know what? I really don't know. I'll have to ask Vance."

"It's my belief," Jillian continued, "that diamond thieves employ high-tech equipment to ... Zachary? What are the dogs doing?"

At that exact moment, both leashes went taut, but that was because both dogs had stopped walking. As I looked back to see what they were doing, I noticed they were both staring up at the open sky. It was then that I noticed we had been out here much longer than I had thought. The sun had set not that long ago, and the sky was getting noticeably darker. Thankfully, the farm's parking lot was just around the corner, so we were in no danger of becoming lost.

That's one thing to be said for being out in the middle of nowhere at night: no light pollution. If you think you've seen it dark before, then I challenge you to drive out to the countryside and see for yourself. It becomes pitch black outside. There are no streetlamps, barely any passing cars, and most houses sit so far back from the road that they're obscured by trees.

Granted, it wasn't that dark yet, but I did notice that some of the brighter stars were starting to appear. Planets, too, for that matter, after spotting Jupiter on the southern horizon, and Venus hanging low in the east. The dogs, however, were staring almost straight up, facing north. What was up there? Well, unless I was very much mistaken, it was the constellation Leo. Had they spotted something? Perhaps they had heard a passing jet?

Jillian stared at the three of us with a bemused expression. "Can you tell what they're looking at?"

"The stars? I don't really see anything else. Guys? Come on. It's getting dark, and we need to go."

The dogs refused to budge. Actually, I don't even think they blinked. Looking back up at the darkening sky, I shrugged. I'm ashamed to say that it's gotten to the point where I don't even question it anymore. If the dogs showed interest in something, then my auto-pilot kicked on and I'd take a few pictures of whatever they were facing. Somehow, and it didn't matter what it was, the pictures would always tie into the case we were working on in some fashion. In this case, they were staring up, at the sky. I didn't know how well my phone could take a picture of the stars, but I figured if it would get the dogs moving, then so be it.

I had just activated my camera app and snapped a picture when a blip of light emerged from the east and streaked west. It was a shooting star! And, I might have even caught that on my phone!

"A shooting star!" Jillian observed. "Look, Zachary. There goes another one!"

Before I knew what was happening, shooting stars were everywhere! They were zinging in from every direction, and occurring every couple of seconds. The burst lasted about five minutes, and resulted in the four of us staring up at the sky with absolute wonder. Still armed with my phone, I started taking photo after photo, with the hopes of getting a few good shots.

"Why would Sherlock and Watson care about shooting stars?" Jillian wondered aloud.

I shrugged. "It has to do with that freakin' diamond, I'm sure. After all, shooting stars are nothing but meteoroids entering our atmosphere. ET was found inside one of those meteorites. It all makes sense, I suppose."

"Seems fairly straightforward," Jillian decided. "Has either of them noticed anything out of the ordinary during this case?"

"Please," I scoffed. "Just about everything is, when it comes to those two. Let's see, off the top of my head, there was the dumpster, but I think that was when we found the stolen pills."

"What else?" Jillian pressed.

"Well, I remember one of the grocery stores had a mylar balloon in it. Sherlock was absolutely fascinated with it. I knew it was connected to the case when I snapped a picture of it and he promptly lost interest."

"Simply amazing," Jillian said.

"The list goes on and on, I'm afraid. Just once, I'd like to solve a case without their help."

"Oh, I'm sure you can do it," Jillian assured me.

Right on cue, both dogs snorted, in unison.

"Thanks for the support, guys. It means the world. Snots."

Jillian laughed, Sherlock gave me his famous stink-eye look, and Watson? She wriggled with delight when I stopped to give her ears a good scratching. Sherlock's scornful look at his pack-mate had me extending Watson's ear scratching by a few more seconds.

"Are you a fan of astronomy?" I eagerly asked.

Jillian nodded. "I am. It's probably why I like sci-fi as much as I do. I love watching the stars. I could lose myself for hours."

"This confirms it," I said, after noticing the amount of meteors appeared to be slowing. "I'm going to get my telescope reassembled."

"You have a telescope?" Jillian asked, impressed. "Do you know what kind?"

I nodded. "As a matter of fact, I do. It's an 8" Schmidt—Cassegrain, on a computerized mount.

If I could ever figure it out, I could get my tablet to interface with it and control what I was looking at with it."

"I'm not sure what 'Cassegrain' means," Jillian said, "but I do know the larger the aperture, the farther it can see. It sounds like you have a powerful telescope."

"The best part is the mount. It's all computerized."

"Which means what, exactly?"

"Once aligned, I can use my tablet to see what the sky looks like from my present location, and automatically tell my telescope to look for a certain object. Planets, nebulae, galaxies; anything that's in the Star Register, it should be able to find it. But, that's not the best part."

"What's the best part?" Jillian eagerly asked.

"You've looked through telescopes before?" I wanted to know.

Jillian nodded. "I have, but they were never computerized. You had to use little knobs to line up the stars."

"Here's an example. Have you ever looked at one of the planets? Like Saturn, or maybe Jupiter?"

"I love Jupiter!" Jillian gushed. "All those pretty colors. I've never used any telescope where our solar system's largest planet hasn't appeared like a bright yellow blob."

"Let me guess. Whenever you got one of the planets lined up, you only had a few moments before the Earth's rotation pulled the telescope away and you had to make some adjustments to bring it back into view?"

Jillian shrugged. "All the time. It's just the way it was. Why do you ask?"

"A computerized mount, when properly aligned and configured, will make all the necessary adjustments to keep whatever you're looking at in the viewfinder."

Jillian's eyes widened with surprise. "Really?"

"Cross my heart. I'll prove it to you as soon as I can."

"You're on, Zachary."

Getting my telescope up and running just jumped to the very top of my priority list.

"Have you thought about where you'd like our wedding to be?" Jillian then asked, as we stopped by the farm's staffed office and reported our tree had been selected.

A farm hand smiled at us, pulled out a two-way radio, and dispatched a team to retrieve the tree. I then remembered the tree was at least 15' tall and quickly looked over at my Jeep. That sucker was most definitely not going to fit.

"Do you guys have a delivery service?" I hesitantly asked.

The young kid nodded. "We're booked up for the rest of the night. We wouldn't be able to get it to you until tomorrow."

I nodded and then pointed back at my car. "Do you see that Jeep there? That's ours. The tree we picked out is over a dozen feet high. Think it'll fit in that?"

The kid laughed. "There's no way, unless you'd like to be cleaning needles out of your upholstery for the next five years."

"Tomorrow will be just fine," Jillian assured the teenager. "I'll give you my address. And please don't worry. I'll be home all day, so you can come at any time."

"There's a switch," the kid softly muttered.

"What is?" I asked.

The kid jumped, as though he had just been caught with his hand in the cookie jar.

"Most people are so impatient," the kid admitted. "It's like people expect to get what they want, exactly when they want it."

"We're in no rush," I assured the kid.

"Says you," Jillian countered, but not before she giggled as she caught sight of the worker's horrified look. "I'm just teasing Zachary. Don't worry, tomorrow will be fine."

After the paperwork had been completed, and the bill paid, we piled back into the Jeep and headed for home. Man alive, was it dark outside. It felt like my headlights were being swallowed up by the darkness.

"So, about our wedding. You had asked me where I think we should have it?"

Jillian nodded. "That's right."

"Well, I'm thinking it should be in Oregon."

Jillian playfully swatted my arm. "No, I mean, would you prefer an inside or an outside wedding?"

"Hmm, I'm sensing I need to say the word 'outside'."

"Good answer, Zachary."

"I take it you'd like to have the ceremony outside?"

Jillian nodded. "I would. Do you have any idea how many members of your family would attend?"

I scratched the side of my head as I carefully navigated my way down the unpaved road. If you thought I was going slow before, then try driving on this type of road at night. I had to be going no faster than 8 mph. We were going to be lucky if we made it home before midnight. "You asked me that a couple of weeks ago. I should have given you an answer then. Umm, the truthful answer is, I'm not sure. My mom tells me that I have relatives in a number of states, only I've never met them. Well, the majority of them. What about you?"

"My family isn't that big," Jillian admitted. "Aside from my brother and my parents, I have one uncle, living in California, and a great-aunt, who lives in Maine, of all places."

"I've been to Maine. Bar Harbor, if you want to get technical."

"What were you doing there?" Jillian wanted to know.

"I was at a lobster bake. From what I have heard, you haven't had lobster until you tried one that was caught earlier in the day."

"Zachary Michael, you told me you don't like lobster!"

"I don't."

"But ... I don't understand."

"I had steak," I clarified.

"Then what were you ...?"

"My publisher has a wicked sense of humor," I calmly stated, as I slowed my Jeep even further as I took a tight, hairpin curve in the road. "You should have seen her laugh once she told me where she was sending me."

"And this was a place called Bar Harbor?"

"Or, as the locals affectionately call it, 'Bah Hahba'."

"They most certainly do not," Jillian giggled.

"They really do. Have you ever been?"

"Not to Bar Harbor, but I have been to the state before. Bangor."

"Home of Stephen King. Nice choice."

My cell began ringing, and since it was currently paired with my Jeep's stereo, I had the ringtone playing at full volume. This time, I had an up-tempo blues type of song blasting out of the speakers: *Shake, Rattle, & Roll*. It was a song that had been released in 1954, and it had been recently assigned to Vance's number.

"I love this song," Jillian gushed.

"Hi, Jillian," Vance's voice suddenly said, as the music was silenced. "I'm assuming he's driving?"

"I'm here," I told my friend.

"What song do you have me under now?" Vance

wanted to know. "As long as it isn't that eardrum-shattering '*We're not gonna take it*', I'm fine."

"Well, it has been the theme song to Peter Pan," I said, which drew a squawk of surprise from my detective friend. "But, Jillian hinted it was kinda rude, so I changed it for you. You're welcome."

"Thank you, Jillian. I owe you a drink."

"And I'll be collecting that drink the next time we all go out to eat," Jillian assured him. "Want to know what Zachary has in place now?"

"I'm gonna regret this, but sure, what the hell. What song is it?"

"*Shake, Rattle, & Roll*, by Big Joe Henry," I answered.

"Huh? Why choose that one?"

"What's the first thing you think of when you hear that song?" I asked.

There were a few seconds of silence as Vance considered. "That you're old and you like your golden oldies?"

Jillian giggled and I shot a dark look at my stereo. "Bite me, pal. It's *Clue*, the movie."

"Oh, that's right! Awesome choice, buddy! I totally take back that snarky comment about the golden oldies."

"Appreciated. What's up?"

"Zack, I thought you should know. The perp who stole ET? He's finally been identified!"

NINE

T his has been one mother of a week," I complained, as I followed Jillian into one of our favorite restaurants in PV. Casa de Joe's may not sound like a very authentic Mexican restaurant, but they had, hands down, the best carne asada burritos in town. And, as long as we're at it, I should expand that to include Medford and Grants Pass, too. "I kid you not, it feels like last Monday happened several weeks ago."

Jillian shrugged. "I didn't think it was that bad. Aside from the difficulty of buying groceries, it hasn't been too inconvenient."

"That's what I'm talking about," I clarified. "After having experienced what an actual panic-buying session is all about, I can thank my lucky stars that I have never purchased an item just because someone else has. I mean, think about it. What if the people all decided that toilet paper would shortly be in demand? And what happens next? People start buying toilet paper, even if they didn't need it. No, it's not worth it."

"Good for you, Zachary," Jillian told me, as she navigated her way through the heavenly smells emanating from the kitchen. "Look. Harry and Julie are already here."

"Hey, bro!" Harry exclaimed, as he stood up. He held out a clenched fist and waited for me to give it a bump. "How's it goin' with your case? Figured out who stole all the cranberries from Gary's Grocery yet? Once you do, pop him a good one for me, will you? If I can't get my spiked cranberry cider this year, then heads are gonna roll."

"You're not getting it this year," Julie confirmed, as she gave me a smile. She looked back at her husband and shook her head. "If you'd like straight cranberry juice, then I can get on board. Otherwise, there'll be no more booze for you."

Harry sighed. "Yes, dear."

"How's the weight-loss going?" I asked, as Jillian and I took seats across from our friends at our table.

"Slow," Harry glumly answered.

"And whose fault is that?" Julie asked. "Who keeps drinking a beer or two behind the house?"

"You know 'bout that?" Harry asked, amazed.

Julie nodded. "I do."

"Uh, dare I ask *how*?"

Julie shook her head and laughed. "Because I can count, Harrison. I know when a beer goes missing. And if you try to blame this on Hardy again, then so help me, you'll be the star of a video which will make Vance's tap-dancing Peter Pan video look tame in comparison."

"They were light beers!" Harry protested. "And I would never pin the blame on our son."

"You already have," Julie countered, as she took a sip of water and sat back in her chair. "You said Hardy must have found your stash and helped himself to a few."

"Like father, like son," I softly quipped.

Overhearing me, Julie nodded. "Sad, but true. I'd like to nip that in the bud as quickly as possible."

"Don't drag him into this," Harry complained. "He's just a kid."

"A kid who has no business drinking," Julie corrected. "But, you're right. This is something we'll talk about once we get home."

Harry groaned softly and returned his attention to his beer. Just then, we heard a loud commotion. Looking up, we saw Vance, Tori, and their two daughters headed our way.

"Hi, girls!" Jillian said. "Are you two hungry?"

"*Muy*," Victoria observed. She was wearing a thick, maroon sweatshirt, blue jeans with rips at the knees, and sparkling, and I do mean *sparkling* ruby red sneakers. Maybe she was going through a Judy Garland phase? "*Yo tengo hambre.*"

"What'd she say?" Harry asked, as he turned to me.

"She's hungry," Jillian translated, after I held my hands up in a helpless manner. "*¿Que quieres comer anoche?*"

JEFFREY POOLE

The brunette teenager blinked a few times as she gaped at my fiancée. "Huh?"

Jillian giggled. "I asked what you want to eat tonight."

The young teen was taken aback. "Oh. Umm ..." Victoria looked at her father. "Did you know what she said?"

Vance nodded. "While not the first phrase I learned, it had to be in the top five. The girls are learning Spanish, in case you didn't know."

"We pieced it together," I said, causing Harry to snort with laughter.

"What was the first phrase you learned?" Jillian curiously asked.

"*¿Donde esta el baño?*" Vance chuckled.

Tiffany, a young, blonde version of her mother, turned to her older sister. "What did he say?"

Victoria snickered. "Daddy asked, 'where's the bathroom'. I think that was the first question I was able to ask."

"Smart kid," I commented, earning me a smile from Vance's oldest daughter.

Jillian turned to Julie. "So, when is your due date again?"

Julie sighed as she sat back in her chair. "December 11th, and let me tell you, it can't get here quickly enough."

"How's this pregnancy going for you?" Tori wanted to know. "Easier or harder than the first two?"

"The first two were a breeze compared to this,"

Julie miserably answered. "With Drew and Hardy, I didn't have a single bit of morning sickness. I was up and moving around until the week before they were born. With this one? It's all I can do to keep anything down and whenever I move, I hurt."

"Well, what do you expect?" Harry said. "You're having twins, babe."

"*We* are having twins," Julie corrected. She gave her husband a stern look. "And whose fault is that?"

"Don't look at me," Harry protested. "You're the one with a history of twins in the family, Jules. There's not one set of twins on my side."

"Harrison, if you ..."

"Are you going to be okay here?" I asked, cutting Harry's wife off. "You must be uncomfortable as hell. If there's someplace else we can go that works better for you, just say so, okay?"

"You're very sweet, Zack," Julie told me, as she shot a dark look at Harry. "Sitting, standing, walking, talking, it doesn't matter. I'm miserable. Don't worry about me. I'll have my glass of water and maybe a few chips."

"She hasn't had much of an appetite in the last month or so," Harry said, by way of explanation.

"But, do I still put on the weight?" Julie grumped. "Of course I do. I can't even begin to imagine how much more weight I'm going to pack on."

Eager to steer the conversation on to a safer subject, I hesitantly cleared my throat. "Do you know what you're going to have? Boys? Girls? One of each? Do you guys have a preference?"

"What if it was three?" Vance sniggered, which earned him a thump in the gut from Tori.

"You shut your filthy little mouth!" Harry all but hissed out. A moment later, he grinned at Vance and then me. "Wouldn't that be something? I think Julie would kill me if the doc announced there was another one in there."

"True story," Julie confirmed. "And, for the record, they are going to be girls."

A round of congratulations erupted. Drinks were lifted, or, as was the case with Julie, glasses of water were lifted, toasts were made, and a few drinks were refilled. Once everyone had placed their orders, Vance clinked his glass a few times.

"No, I'm not giving a speech," my friend began, as he stared at the multitude of eager faces. "I thought I could give an update on what I had found out today."

"I want to know about the perp," I began. "You announced last night that you knew who it was. I've been waiting all day for this, so, spill."

"His name is Peter Grant," Vance began.

"Peter Grant?" Harry repeated, as he frowned. "Not what I had pictured, bro."

"You and me both," I confirmed. "Well, what can you tell us about him?"

"He's 24, and an intern at the laboratory."

"Observatory," Tori quietly corrected.

Vance frowned. "Whatever. Anyway, he's a 4.0

GPA grad student with no criminal background whatsoever."

"Then, what the hell possessed him to steal that diamond?" I wanted to know. "From the sounds of things, this is a good kid we're talking about."

"Was a good kid," Harry corrected.

"Are you sure you have the right guy?" Jillian quietly asked. "How certain are you of your source?"

"100%," Vance reported. "This info came straight from the guys at Jacobsen. They ..."

"Jacobsen?" Harry interrupted, as he held up his hands in a time-out gesture.

"Sorry. It's the name of the observatory. Now, as I was saying, Jacobsen is the one who provided the info. They checked their people and discovered one of them was missing."

"This intern," I guessed.

Vance nodded. "Right. He's not answering his cell, he hasn't shown up for work, and his family hasn't heard from him in days."

"Why reveal the name now?" Jillian asked. "This theft happened, what, over a week ago, right?"

Vance consulted his notebook. "That's right. And, to answer your question, Jillian, this was at the University's request. The captain managed to put me in touch with the head of their astronomy department. They didn't want to air any of the university's dirty laundry, if you catch my meaning. However, since no new leads were appearing, and they are now in danger of losing several grants if they don't get that diamond back, they're quickly becoming desperate."

"Meaning, it's time to appeal to the masses," Julie observed.

"Exactly. They're appealing to the public for information. Last I heard, they're including free lifetime passes to the observatory if any tips are produced which lead to an arrest."

Jillian started to raise a hand, and sensing an opportunity to give her some good-natured ribbing, I pushed it down.

"You're not in school, dear."

Jillian giggled and swatted my arm away. Then, she raised it again. "Vance? I have a question."

"And Ms. Cooper has the floor," Vance said, giving her a mock bow.

"Has the police department considered the possibility that Peter might have been blackmailed? What if he was forced to steal that diamond?"

"It was considered," Vance admitted.

"And?" Jillian prompted.

"It was dismissed."

"Why? How can they be so sure?"

"We have Zack to thank for that," Vance announced. "I see a lot of blank faces, including Zack's. All right, I'll show you what I mean. Who has the largest phone?"

I looked over at Jillian before returning my

gaze to Vance. "What was that?"

Vance held up his hands and created a rectangular shape with the thumb and index finger from each hand. "Who's got the phone with the biggest screen?"

Julie, in the midst of drinking from her glass of water, snorted, which ended up causing her to make a mess down the front of her shirt. She reached for a napkin, but not before hooking a thumb in Harry's direction.

"Him."

"I do not," Harry protested.

"Are you kidding?" Julie sputtered. "That screen is so big, it could be used as a tablet."

"Well, I like watching videos on it," Harry reluctantly admitted. "I have to be able to see it, don't I?"

Vance nodded. "Perfect. Can I see it?"

"What for?" Harry suspiciously asked, as he pulled his cell from an inside jacket pocket.

Amazed whistles sounded from all around the table. Julie hadn't been kidding. The screen on that monster had to be at least 7", from corner to corner. The town vet looked lovingly down at his phone before reluctantly passing it over.

"Look, pal, I'm not gonna destroy it," Vance grumbled. "I just want to show you something. Okay. Here's the website that Zack pulled up yesterday. He's the one who informed us that there had been a theft up in Washington State."

"You want us to watch a news story?" Harry

querulously asked.

"No. Well, yes. You'll see what I mean. Here it is. Now, do you see this? These buildings back here?"

There was a chorus of acknowledgements from the table. I waited, as I knew which part of the video Vance wanted us to see. And there it was. In the background, a semi appeared, hauling a long, open trailer with a large red mound visible in the back.

Vance tapped the screen, which caused the video to pause itself. "Here it is. This truck? It's hauling cranberries. Do you see those buildings back there? That's the cranberry processing plant. Peter obviously knew it was over there, which suggests premeditation, so ... Jillian? Do you have something you want to add?"

"What if this Peter Grant person is exactly like he seems? A good person who made a bad decision? He has the diamond ..."

"... ET," I quietly offered.

"Right," Vance said. "He has ET in his possession, he knows he has to get rid of it should he be caught, but doesn't know what to do with it. We know he's smart, since we confirmed he has a 4.0 GPA. Do we know why he went over to the plant? Did he have an accomplice? I can't imagine the plant would let a complete stranger have access to their machines."

"Seems more spur of the moment to me," Julie suggested.

"Me, too," I decided. "What I'd like to know

is, from the time this Peter fellow leaves the observatory, how soon before he's at the processing plant? If it was almost immediately, then that would suggest it was part of his plan. If not, and let's say he lingers outside while he's trying to figure out what to do, then that would suggest there was no forethought into his visit to the plant."

Vance handed Harry's phone back before pulling out his own. "I'm sure I can find out. Give me a moment, okay?"

"You can do that later, pal," I said. "You're off duty. You don't need to ..."

"It's okay," Vance assured me. He started to dial when he noticed Tori nodding her head toward the front door. "I'll be right back."

"What's with this plant, anyway?" Harry suddenly asked. "You guys have brought it up several times now. What's the big deal?"

The entire table fell silent, and that included Victoria and Tiffany.

"What?" Harry demanded. "Did I miss something?"

"You do know that there's been a rash of grocery store burglaries, right?" I asked my friend. He gave me a non-committal shrug, causing an evil thought to occur. Was he confused or was that the expression he typically wore? Deciding to give him the benefit of the doubt, I let the matter drop. "Someone has been stealing cranberries, of all things."

"What?" Harry sputtered. "From other stores

besides Gary's? You're kidding! I mean, I like a good cranberry cocktail, just like everyone else, but I don't like it that much."

"Don't you read the newspaper?" I incredulously asked.

"Hey, I've been busy," Harry sputtered. "I've been putting in long hours at the clinic *and* getting a nursery ready, bro. Cut me a little slack, all right?"

I had to give him that one. "Fine, you're forgiven."

"What other stores were hit?" Harry wanted to know.

"Grants Pass was burglarized first," Tori reported. "Then Medford, and finally, PV."

"Actually," I slowly began, "three other stores were hit in rapid succession first. Gold Beach, Port Orford, and Klamath."

"Klamath Falls," Jillian corrected, "and I did not know that."

"Right. Thanks. Those three were hit first, and then Vance figured out the perp probably had to expand his search when he couldn't find his diamond."

"Is that why Gary's entire supply of baby formula was stolen?" Jillian asked. "We were made to think the thief was interested in something besides cranberries?"

I nodded. "We think they were nothing more than diversions. Formula here in PV, drugs in Grants Pass, and booze in Medford."

Vance returned at that moment, and none of us could mistake the grin on his face.

"Good news?" I hopefully asked. "Did you find what you were looking for?"

My detective friend nodded. "You guys need to listen to this. Peter Grant? He has a roommate."

"Most students living on campus do," Jillian said.

Vance nodded. "Right, but how many of those roommates just so happen to have girlfriends who work at a cranberry processing plant?"

The table fell silent.

"That rules out blackmail," I decided. "Peter obviously knew about the plant next door. He clearly knew his roommate's girlfriend worked there, and therefore, had an 'in' at the plant. Let me guess. This girlfriend? Does she work in the area that handles the packaging?"

Vance nodded. "You're close. She works in shipping. Well, at least, she *did*. Once the plant learned about their unauthorized visitor, it took them all of about five minutes to review the security footage and find out who allowed Peter inside the facility."

"Did they say how long she has worked there?" I asked.

Vance consulted his notes. "Not long. Three months. She was hired, along with a number of other seasonal workers, to help during the harvest. They do it every year."

Jillian had pulled out her phone and was studying it intently. After a few moments, she looked up and waggled her phone.

"In case anyone was wondering, mid-September through early November is when cranberries are harvested."

"Here's what I think happened," Vance began. "This Peter fellow sees an opportunity to steal this special diamond …"

"… ET," several voices interrupted.

"Yeah, right. ET. Phone home, right? Whatever. Now, Peter takes possession of ET but realizes he won't be able to hold on to it long, so he tries to find a way to hide it. Officials at Jacobsen confirm the intern was only left alone for about 15 minutes, so during that time, Peter takes the diamond and flees outside."

"Is there any security footage?" Jillian asked.

Vance nodded. "Thanks for bringing that up. Yeah, I was told the footage was reviewed, and security was able to follow Peter through the observatory, until he made it outside. Once there, they lost sight of him, but we've pretty much figured out where he went."

"The cranberry plant," Julie added.

"Right, he headed straight for the plant. Now, I've been in contact with the people who run the plant. They do have a few cameras in there, but not many. They can confirm Peter Grant arrived at the building about ten minutes after he left the observatory, but that's it.

"Once inside the processing plant, Peter heads

straight for the one person he knows: his roommate's girlfriend, who conveniently enough, works in shipping. I figure Peter either saw the passing bags of cranberries and dropped the diamond in, or else added it to the bin of berries that were in the process of being bagged. Regardless of how he introduced the gem to the cranberries, ET was sealed up and shipped out. Now, what he did next was truly clever."

"*What* was clever?" I wanted to know.

"I'm guessing, since Peter's acquaintance worked in the shipping department, he had to have found out where that particular batch of berries was heading, namely MDC, which we know is in Medford."

"And MDC happens to supply all the small stores in the southwestern section of the state," I quietly added. "Once you add that in, it starts to make sense."

"So," Vance continued, "armed with the knowledge that his diamond was headed for MDC, Peter realizes he needs to find out which store will end up with his diamond."

"The observatory's diamond," Jillian and I both corrected.

"Right, whatever. Now, this is where Peter is hit with the first flaw in his plan: MDC didn't have specific boxes going to specific stores. Instead, they simply had a supply and demand system set up and filled orders as they were received."

"That explains the number of stores that were

hit," Julie decided. "He didn't know where ET was going to end up."

"Right," Vance confirmed. "I was able to call MDC and get someone from administration on the phone. The lady I talked to confirmed that someone called them last week and asked them about shipments of cranberries. Thinking nothing of it, she informed the person which stores were getting deliveries on which dates."

"Have any other stores been hit since Gary's?" I asked.

The table fell silent as everyone present considered the question.

"No," Vance said, shaking his head. "Captain Nelson agrees with you, Zack. He thinks the diamond must have been in one of the bags that were destined for PV."

"Then, it's probably long gone," Tori guessed.

There was a collective groan as the majority of the people at our table agreed. I, on the other hand, was shaking my head.

"I think it's still here, in PV."

Four different conversations came to an abrupt end.

"What was that, pal?" Vance asked.

"I think ET is still here, somewhere," I repeated. "Or, at the very least, within our grasp to get it back."

Suddenly, I had everyone's attention. Vance gave me a hard look. "Explain that."

Tori's hand appeared, and was quickly slapped

down, over Vance's.

"*Please*," Vance hastily amended, as he gave his wife an apologetic smile.

"Sherlock and Watson," I announced. "They still think they're working a case. Now, of all the cases we've worked together, after a case has been closed, have they ever kept looking at various things?"

"No," Vance immediately answered. "What have they been looking at?"

Right then, the waitress was back, wheeling a cart piled high with steaming dishes of aromatic food. We all waited to be given our orders, and once the waitress had departed, I pulled out my phone. Opening my Photos app, I held it up for Vance to see.

"Well, there's no time like the present to go over the Corgi Clues. Does anyone have any objections to listening to me prattle off what the dogs have been interested in this time around?" When no one said anything, I nodded appreciatively. "All righty, let's see what we have. Here we go. This is the first picture I took. Can everyone see it?"

"What are we looking at?" Julie asked, from across the table. "Is that a dumpster? Did you take a picture of some trash?"

"Yes and no," I explained. I zoomed in on the duffel bag. "See this bag? This was stuffed full of meds."

"Taken from the first store to be hit?" Harry asked. "Was that Gold Beach, bro?"

"The first three didn't have diversions in place," I explained, which drew a nod from Vance. "This is from Grants Pass. Their pharmacy was hit, and tons of prescription pills were taken, only Sherlock and Watson found them in a nearby dumpster. This is the first crime scene we were asked to visit."

"That doesn't make any sense, bro," Harry said, confused. "Those drugs probably had a significant street value to them."

"Which is how we knew it was a diversion," Vance added. "Go on, Zack.

"Right. Okay, picture two is … the same thing. Moving on. So is picture three. Here we go. Pictures four and five show the freezer door at the Grants Pass grocery."

"Why?" Julie asked.

I shrugged. "This was the first store to be hit. I can only assume the dogs were bringing our attention to the fact that something else was off."

The next photograph appeared on my phone. I heard Victoria and Tiffany giggle as it became apparent I had taken a picture of a helium-filled mylar balloon. This one was flower-shaped, and had Happy 7th Birthday! festooned across the front. At a loss, I looked at Vance and helplessly held up my hands.

"I'm at a loss on this one. Thoughts?"

"Happy 7th Birthday," Jillian read. "Was someone turning seven?"

"Not that I know of," I said.

"Is the number seven relevant somehow?" Tori asked.

"We don't know," Vance confessed. "It'll make sense eventually. Moving on, Zack."

"Roger that. Okay, after the balloon, we have a picture of a kid wearing a backpack. What in the world?"

"Isn't that Colin?" Jillian asked, as she leaned over my shoulder to look at the picture.

I snapped my fingers. "Right. I remember now. We were at the florist, and you and Hannah were talking about something flower-related. That's when I saw Colin sitting by himself. That's when I challenged him to a Robotron throw down."

"Robotron, the arcade game?" Harry asked, interested. "Dude, I could take you down any day of the week."

"Please," I scoffed. "Robotron is my game. I'd dip your butt in Pine-Sol and wipe the floor with you."

Harry's eyes narrowed. "It's on, bro."

Vance held up his hands in a time-out gesture. "Guys? Focus. Now, Zack, do we know why you took a picture of Colin or his backpack?"

"No. Your guess is as good as mine."

"Hmm. We'll come back to that one. What's next?"

"Let's see. Ah, here we go. We have a picture of a rack full of numbers and letters."

"Are they stencils?" Tori asked, as she leaned forward for a better look.

Vance shook his head. "No, I remember this now. These were adhesive numbers and letters, the kind you'd affix to a mailbox if you want to put your address on it."

"Not all the numbers and letters are there," Jillian pointed out. "Zachary? You appear to have zoomed in on the letter F. Do you remember what you were trying to capture?"

"Not a clue. They stopped and stared, I took a picture, and then we moved off. End of story. Do you see anything that stands out?"

"Well, there are some 7s, 9s, and Bs, Cs, and Fs. They're out of 8s, As, and Es. How that helps us, I don't know."

"We'll come back to that," I announced, as I slid my finger across the screen and then showed everyone what appeared. "Here we have ... swell. Here we have more trash. It looks like the inside of another trash can. Vance? Do you remember this one?"

I passed my phone to Vance, who studied the picture for so long that he had to tap the screen to prevent the smartphone from going to sleep. "Well, this could be ... wait. This was taken in Medford."

"How can you be sure?" I asked, as I took my phone back.

"Look at the picture, buddy. There are a few wrappers in there, and they're all in Spanish."

"El Gato," I recalled, as I gave my friend a grin. "Got it."

"El Gato?" Jillian repeated, puzzled.

"It's the store that was hit in Medford."

"Ah. Was there something about the trash you wanted to capture?"

"The corgis wouldn't leave the trash can alone," I recalled. "I took the photo just to shut them up."

"Then, it has to be important," Jillian decided. "Oh, look! Zachary? Do you see this, here? It's a cranberry!"

"Coincidence?" I asked.

Vance shook his head. "With your dogs? I doubt it. What else do you got? What's that?"

The next picture on my phone was of the hand-held device the young son of Jillian's landscaper had been holding. He had been playing it while Jillian's yard was being serviced. That game, if memory served, had been available at the arcade where I grew up. It was a blow-em-up type of game, set in space, where the player is at the controls of a one-man fighter, and your only job is to stay alive. Stay alive long enough and you'll join an assault on the bad guys' home base.

"It's the video game a boy was playing outside, at Jillian's, while her yard was being cleaned. Sherlock and Watson had been staring at the boy, only it was revealed later that they were only interested in the game he had been holding. So, I took a picture."

"What game is it?" Jillian wanted to know.

"An old space fighter game," I explained. "The

version I played, at the arcade back home, had this sit-down version where it replicated being in a cockpit, I guess. It cost two quarters to play, and I *sucked* at it."

This brought a round of laughter.

"Another one we'll come back to," Vance decided. "Moving on. What's next?"

I swiped a finger across the screen and shrugged. "Greeting cards, only they look like they're for kids. I can see Darth Vader on one and Yoda on another."

Vance nodded. "Star Wars. Okay. Does anyone know how that fits into the picture?"

The detective was met with silence.

"Moving on. What's next, Zack?"

I stared at the next set of pictures for a few moments as I tried to figure out what I had been trying to take a picture of. Pages of text? Printed pages of text, if you want to get technical. What was … oh. That took a little longer than I would have liked to admit. This was back in Gary's Grocery.

"Shipping invoices," I announced, as I showed the picture to the group. "Why, or how, that's important is beyond me, I'm sorry to say."

"Shipping invoices," Vance repeated, as he took my phone to study the images for himself. "This was, what, two days ago, wasn't it?"

"Right. I figure the dogs perked up because it was yet another reference to a shipment of cranberries, and Gary told us that his entire order of the berries had been taken."

Some soft ooohs and aaahs echoed throughout the room. After a few moments, when no more questions were forthcoming, I moved on to the next set. Looking down at the display, I broke out in a grin. They were the pictures I had taken of our excursion to pick out a Christmas tree yesterday. Surprisingly, the nighttime pictures had turned out quite well!

"Jillian and I headed out yesterday to ..." I trailed off as I realized the amount of crap I was probably going to be given, especially by this particular group of friends, if I revealed what we had been doing. Steeling myself, I took a deep breath and just spit it out. "... pick out a Christmas tree."

Harry snorted with surprise. "It's not even Thanksgiving, bro."

"I know, Harry. Jillian's family is used to decorating early."

"Now, *that* is a good idea," Tori decided, as she looked over at her husband. A knowing smile appeared on her face, which had Vance groaning with dismay. Tori looked back at my fiancée and nodded. "Where did you guys go?"

"To the Mansons," Jillian said, by way of explanation.

"I haven't purchased a tree from them in a few years," Tori said. "Neither of us have anything planned for Saturday. I think we'll head up there and pick out a tree, too. Thanks for the idea, Jillian!"

"You're more than welcome," Jillian said.

"Yeah, thanks, pal," Vance quietly grumbled.

I grinned at my detective friend and gave him a mock salute. I then held up my phone and waggled it.

"This last set of pictures are obviously from yesterday," I said, as I rotated my phone so that the display was facing out. "I …"

"Are those shooting stars?" Tori asked, incredulous. "Zack, you should submit those to a magazine, or something. Those look really cool!"

"We lucked out, that's for sure," I recalled, as I gave Jillian's hand a squeeze. "This happened near the end of the trip. We had selected a tree, arranged for the delivery, and then stepped back outside. Both dogs then stopped and looked up at the stars. When they didn't budge, I decided to humor them, like I usually do, and took a picture, only I took it just as soon as the first shooting star appeared."

Victoria held out her hand, hoping I'd give her the phone so she could have a better look. Once I did, and she and her sister fawned over them for a few minutes, she passed it back.

"How did you get so many shots of the shooting stars?" Tiffany quietly asked me.

"Those pictures don't do it justice," I told the girl. "There were so many stars shooting by us that it was rather hard to miss. It lasted about five minutes, and there had probably been at least a couple hundred shooting stars altogether."

"Meteoroids," Victoria proudly announced. "They're not really shooting stars, but meteoroids."

"Don't you mean meteorites?" Vance hesitantly asked his oldest daughter.

"No, dad. Meteoroids are what you call objects falling through space. A meteorite is what they're called if they strike the Earth."

I had to admit, I had heard the term before, but I never thought I would have it explained to me by a 13-year-old teenager.

"Nicely done," Tori praised. "Someone has been paying attention to her science class. I'm proud of you, Vicki."

The teenager flushed with embarrassment. "Thanks, Mom."

"Do you like astronomy?" Jillian asked the girl.

Victoria nodded. My fiancée then pointed at me. "So do I. So does Zachary. In fact, Zachary has a big, fancy telescope in his garage that he's going to have reassembled. Once he does, I'm sure he'd love to show it to you."

The girl brightened with interest.

"The telescope," I quietly mused. "That reminds me of something."

"What?" Jillian asked.

"I obviously go through the garage whenever I'm getting in or out of the Jeep," I began. "On several occasions, I've noticed Sherlock and Watson staring at something in the garage, and I'm quite certain it's the trunk where I'm storing that telescope. Coincidence?"

"That word doesn't belong in your vocabulary," Vance informed me. "At least, not where your dogs are concerned. They were interested in a telescope? That's not too surprising. After all, we're talking about an extraterrestrial diamond."

I made a point of placing my cell back in my pocket. Because I knew it'd garner a few laughs, I adopted my 'old British dude' persona. "There you have it, ladies and gents. The evidence has been placed before you. What do you make of it?"

Vance snorted with laughter. "Well, we can easily see the references to the cranberries. And the telescope? Obviously meant to refer to outer space."

"Colin's backpack?" I pressed. "The gardener's kid? Or, more specifically, his game?"

"That game is set in outer space," Vance pointed out. "No big surprise there." His cell started to ring. "Hang on a sec. Hello? Yes, this is Detective Vance Samuelson. I ... what's that? You found what? Well, it's a start, I guess. Thank you for letting me know. I'll run it by my consultants and see what ... yes, those consultants. Yes, I'll give Sherlock and Watson a pat for you. Thank you. You have yourself a good evening."

"A fan of the dogs?" I guessed.

"That was Brigitte," Vance explained. "She's new, and has only been manning the front desk for a few weeks now. She was told to pass on a message to me. Zack? They dug into Peter Grant's life and found what they're calling a 'faint' connection to PV."

This got everyone's attention, including myself.

"Oh? Whatcha got, buddy?"

"Peter Grant has a former classmate who is currently living here, in Pomme Valley."

"Where?" Harry wanted to know.

"On G Street," Vance reported.

Right about then, I noticed my fiancée reach for my phone. Having long since programmed one of her fingerprints into my phone's memory, she unlocked it and brought up the pictures. Silently, she flipped through the last two dozen or so before she stopped. Studying the image intently, she then moved to a different image. After a few moments of silence, Jillian excitedly turned to me, and then reached across the table to tap Vance's hand.

"Vance? I think you'd better get out to that former classmate's house, on the double. You are probably going to want to hurry!"

Vance stared at her for a few seconds. "Why?"

"Because Zachary is right. Peter Grant is still in PV, and I'm pretty sure he's currently hiding at his classmate's house!"

TEN

Y ou are going to have to explain yourself," Vance calmly told Jillian. "You think Peter is hiding out at his former classmate's place? Sure, there's a mathematical chance that could happen, but what I want to know is, why do you sound so certain Peter Grant is there?"

Still holding my phone, Jillian spun it around to show me what she was looking at, which was, surprisingly enough, the mylar flower balloon. The Happy 7th Birthday balloon, if you want to get technical. I took my phone back and stared at the picture. Vance rose to his feet and stood behind me so that he, too, could study the photograph.

"What are we looking at besides a balloon?" he wanted to know.

I gave him my phone. "Not a clue. Maybe someone is celebrating their seventh birthday? I don't know."

Jillian stretched out a hand. She wanted the phone back.

"And then there's this one."

We were now looking at the picture I took of the hardware aisle at El Gato, in Medford. I looked at the hanging numbers and letters and then looked back at her with a healthy dose of skepticism on my face.

"I think you're gonna have to throw us a lifeline, my dear."

"The number seven," Jillian explained. "I think that's what the dogs were looking at in this picture."

"The number seven," Vance slowly repeated, "and a balloon with Happy 7th Birthday on it. What about it?"

Just then, Tori gave a visible start. She then smiled at Jillian and then back at me. "You have yourself one smart cookie there."

"Don't I know it. Jillian? What's so special about the seven?"

"What is the seventh letter of the alphabet?" Jillian asked, as though she was addressing a classroom full of students.

Vance, Harry, and I immediately started ticking off letters on our fingers as we worked our way up.

"G," Julie reported. "Oh! Didn't you say that Peter's classmate lived off of G Street?"

"I'll be a monkey's uncle," Vance muttered. He checked his watch, and then looked apologetically at his wife, who promptly pointed at Vance's plate.

"Finish your food, then you can go play."

You would have thought Vance was eating the last meal he was ever going to have. He scarfed his dinner down and looked over at me. For the record, I'm a quick eater. I'd been done for a few minutes.

"Go," Tori laughed. "Go catch the bad guy."

In response, Vance looked over at Jillian, who wore the same expression on her face. "It's okay. Take Zack. Be safe."

I gave my sweetie a quick kiss before I hastily pushed away from the table and hurried to catch up to Vance.

"I think we should pick up the dogs," my detective friend announced, as we left the restaurant's parking lot. "Just in case."

"That's fine by me. Sherlock and Watson would love to spread some of their DNA in here."

Vance swept an arm around the insides of his car. "This is a 1984 Cutlass Supreme. It's the finest vehicle Oldsmobile made with a diesel engine."

"But, it's beige!" I protested. "You really ought to trade this thing in."

"I love this car," Vance argued.

"What kind of gas mileage do you get?"

"In its prime, it got a whopping 19 miles per gallon."

"And now?" I cautiously asked, knowing there was no way in hell it could be maintaining that level of efficiency.

"I don't know. Maybe 10?"

"Listen to that engine. You said this beast is a

diesel?"

Vance shrugged. "So?"

"How many horses does this thing have?"

"A record-shattering 105. So, do you really think I'm concerned with what happens to this car?"

"Then, why not get rid of it and get something newer?" I asked.

"There's no car payment on this baby," Vance proudly informed me.

"There's no car payment on my Jeep, either," I pointed out. "And it's, what, thirty years newer?"

"Yeah, yeah. You sound like Tori."

Twenty minutes later, we were speeding toward G Street, with the dogs happily lounging in the back seat. According to my navigation app on my phone, the address we were headed to was on the northeastern side of town. In fact, the dogs and I frequent this part of town, usually two to three times a week. Why? Well, G Street happens to be the western border of PV's second largest park. Being the closest park to the winery, this is where we typically end up when the dogs need to burn off some energy.

We pulled up to a single-story rambler, which was directly across the street from some type of daycare center. The house was neat, tidy, and had a freshly mown lawn. The first thing I thought of, after studying the house for a few moments, was that whoever lived there must've been a responsible homeowner, since the house looked like it had been well-cared for.

Vance briefly glanced at the house with the low-pitched roof before he beckoned me to join him.

"What about the dogs?" I quietly asked.

"We don't need them yet. Will they be okay in the car?"

I looked through the windows into the sedan's back seat. Both corgis were sprawled out, awake for the time being, but I'd say only moments away from falling asleep.

"They're fine. But, I don't want to leave them out here by themselves for too long."

"Gotcha. Let's go."

"Are we really allowed to do this? I mean, don't we need a warrant?"

"Already phoned it in. Captain Nelson is trying to get a judge to sign off on it."

"Just because of the clues Sherlock and Watson found?"

"If the captain manages to reach Judge Warren first, then we'll have that warrant in no time."

"How can you be so certain?"

"Because the judge is a fan of the dogs. She's an ardent admirer. Are you ready? Let's do this."

Together, we approached the front door. Vance readied his police ID and, with his hand resting on the butt of his revolver, knocked on the door.

"Stephen Carlson, my name is Vance Samuelson. I'm a detective with the Pomme Valley police department. Are you home?"

No answer.

Not to be deterred, Vance tried again, and this time, he knocked harder. Right then, I detected movement in my peripheral vision. Something had moved, and it was on my right. Glancing that way, I saw that the curtains covering the front window were slightly swaying. Someone had just peeked through!

"There's someone here," I urgently whispered. "I think our friend Mr. Carlson just looked out the window."

"How do you know?" Vance quietly asked.

"The curtain just moved. Someone had to have just looked out."

"We know you're in there. Please open up, Mr. Carlson."

We heard someone fumbling on the other side of the door, and then heard a chain rattle a few times, as though it had been unhooked and was now swinging back and forth, striking the door as it did so. The front door cracked open and a tall, thin guy in his mid-twenties peered out at us. He was wearing a cherry red shirt with a white circle on the chest. Inside the circle was what looked like a rectangle with a spike driven through it, resulting in a skewed rectangle. I knew it was a logo for something, but for what, I didn't know.

"Yes?"

"Didn't you hear me knocking before?" Vance pleasantly asked the homeowner. I couldn't help but notice a tiny bit of frustration had crept into his voice.

"Uh, no, sorry. I was playing a video game. Had my headphones on."

"Uh-huh. Listen, as I said, my name is Detective Vance Samuelson. This is Zack Anderson, a consultant for the police. We're here investigating the possibility that a former acquaintance of yours, one Peter Grant, could be here."

"Wh-who?"

Vance's eyes narrowed. My friend clearly wasn't buying Stephen's performance.

"Peter Grant. He was a former classmate of yours."

"Peter. Yeah, I knew him in high school, but not well. What's the matter? Has he done something wrong?"

"He's wanted for questioning in the disappearance of a valuable artifact, stolen from Jacobsen Observatory in Washington State."

"And you think he's here?" Stephen scoffed. "Please. I haven't seen or heard from Peter in years. I'm sorry you've wasted your time."

Stephen started to duck back inside and shut the door, but before he could, Vance jammed his foot forward, which kept the door from closing.

"Mind if we come in to look around?"

"Got a warrant?" Stephen asked, although if you were to ask me, it was a little defensive.

"Not yet," Vance stated. "And I stress the word *yet*. If you're hiding something, Mr. Carlson, now would be a good time to get in front of it. If you turn us away, when we just want to look around, then we're going to be back with every cop in the city. Is that what you want?"

"But, I haven't done anything wrong!" Stephen protested. His voice had risen to a whine, and he was fidgeting from one leg to the other. "What are you looking for?"

"Evidence someone else has been here," Vance answered. "How many people live here?"

"Well ..." Stephen slowly began.

"And I should point out that I already know the answer to this one," Vance dryly added.

"... just me," the homeowner hastily finished.

"Good answer. Now, may we come inside?"

Stephen Carlson reluctantly stepped away from the door. Without waiting to see if he'd have a change of heart, Vance strode inside. Not wanting to be excluded, I hastily followed my detective friend into the house.

The inside of the house was just as impeccable as the outside. Yes, the house was neat, it didn't smell, and I couldn't find a speck of dust anywhere. However, the décor of the place was something else.

This was the home of someone who was a fan of comic books and movies. And by fan, I mean *super-fan*. I saw glass display cases with strange, costumed figurines inside. I saw several comic books, sealed in protective acrylic sleeves. There was even a collection of swords on the far wall, and because I was a sci-fi fan, I could easily pick out

Bilbo Baggins' sword, Sting; the sword wielded by Aragorn in the *Lord of the Rings* trilogy; and there was a life-sized replica of a Scottish Claymore, undoubtedly from the movie *Braveheart*. Models of spaceships sat on shelves, and I could see several signed pictures hanging on the wall.

No wonder the house looked so neat. Whatever this guy did for a living, he clearly made enough money to pay for a housekeeper and a gardener. Judging from the pale skin this guy had, I don't think he spent any time outdoors at all.

"What do you do for a living?" Vance asked. I could tell my friend was trying to keep things casual and, hopefully, put this nerdy-looking guy at ease. "I like some of your collectibles in here."

"Like you know what this stuff is," Stephen scoffed. "These pieces are for serious collectors. And I'm an accountant."

"I personally love that Sting sword," I said, as I grinned at the guy. "I love anything from Middle Earth."

Stephen's face lit up. His hesitation was gone, as was the cold shoulder he had been giving us.

"If you think that's cool, then you should check out that display case over there. Recognize what's in it?"

I glanced in the direction Stephen had been pointing. "It looks like Bilbo's ring. Or Frodo's, if you want to get technical."

"It's an authentic replica," Stephen proudly declared. "Cost me $149.95."

"What a nerd," I heard Vance softly grumble. I elbowed him in the stomach to shut him up.

Vance began to wander around the living room. Catching sight of the kitchen, he started in that direction when a loud clatter had both of us turning around. Stephen was there, on his hands and knees, hastily scraping a spilled stack of some type of cards back into a case.

"Sorry. I'm a bit clumsy."

"What are those?" I curiously asked. "Baseball cards?"

"Oh, heavens no. These are the serial killer cards that were used in the *Addams Family* movie, particularly by Wednesday Addams' little friend, Joel."

"You certainly know your movies," I observed, amazed. "And are these the actual cards used on screen?"

"Well, no, they're replicas," Stephen admitted. "Hey! You don't need to go in there. The kitchen is a mess."

It was too late. Vance was standing in the kitchen and slowly turning in a circle. He looked over at Stephen and crossed his arms over his chest.

"Are you baking something, Mr. Carlson? Perhaps, something with cranberries?"

"Cranberries?" I repeated, as I frowned. "Where'd you manage to find those? My fiancée needs some and I can't find a bag of those berries to save my soul."

"Er, maybe I have a bag you could have?" Stephen anxiously told me. "I, er, have a tendency to buy more than I can use. Let me check my freezer."

I walked through the open archway and entered the kitchen. My eyes widened with surprise as I took in no fewer than five empty bags of cranberries. Three were scattered across the counter and two were in the sink. Vance caught my eye. That's when I noticed he was holding his phone. Right then, my phone chirped like a cricket. It's a strange tone to have assigned to incoming texts, I know, but I kinda like it.

CHECK TRASH OUTSIDE

I nodded. "Stephen? I'll be right back. I have my dogs in the car and I just need to be certain they're okay."

"Uh, sure. No problem."

To maintain the illusion, Vance tossed me the keys as I hurried outside. I checked the sides of the house for a trash can, but naturally, I came up short. Maybe they were stored in the garage? There was one way to find out.

I let the dogs out of Vance's car and was immediately pulled to the garage. Yep, the trash cans had to be in there, and what were the chances they'd be full of discarded cranberry bags? About to text Vance that there were no trash cans outside, I paused. Damned if I didn't just tilt my head, like a dog who had heard a curious noise.

I had just heard a window sliding open, and from the sounds of it, it was close. A clattering followed, suggesting that whoever had opened it just pushed the screen loose and let it fall to the ground. Flattening myself against the side of the house, I waited to see who, or what, had made the noise. Then, I heard a soft thud, as if someone had jumped from the window and landed just around the corner from me. Stepping away from the garage door, I came face-to-face with a surprised young guy who was dressed in a dark brown shirt that had a bandolier printed across the chest, stretching from the left shoulder down to the right hip, and a pair of khakis. An odd mix, I remember thinking, but the geeky-looking kid managed to pull it off. He took one look at me, let out a squawk of surprise, and immediately sprinted down the driveway and out onto the street.

Remembering I had Vance's keys, I tossed them by the sedan's front driver's wheel and took off after the kid. It had to be Peter Grant. Who else would have run away like that? Especially coming from this house?

Since I had been on several foot pursuits before, I already knew that my ability to carry on a conversation dwindled rapidly the longer I was running. Quickly dialing Vance, I gave Sherlock and Watson as much slack on their leash as I could, and started running.

"Zack? What are you ..."

"Vance! I'm in pursuit! Peter Grant was there, and he snuck out of the house while I was outside!"

"You rock, Zack! I ... *you've got my keys!*"

"N-no ... threw th-them by th-the front wheel ..."

"Don't have a heart attack, buddy. I'm heading outside now. Yes! I see my keys! Where are you?"

"H-h-heading u-up G ..."

"Roger that. Have you passed Pinetop yet?"

"J-just d-did."

It felt like my lungs were on fire. I couldn't catch my breath, my legs felt like lead, and I'm honestly surprised I didn't keel over and collapse. Seriously, what was the point of putting all that time and energy on my stupid tread-climber when I sounded like a chain-smoking asthmatic after only thirty seconds of running? It was embarrassing.

I heard an engine approach. Thankful that Vance had been able to catch up to me in a matter of moments, I turned to wave him down, only the car I was staring at did not belong to my friend. I was looking at a very familiar Corvette Stingray. Behind the wheel, and looking at me with a wide-eyed expression, was Dottie.

The 'Vette skidded to a stop and Dottie leapt out of the driver's seat.

"Zack? Are you okay? What's going on?"

"C-can I g-get a r-ride? Ch-chasing s-suspect."

"You're chasing someone? And you want me to drive? Omigod! This is the best day ever! Sure, hop in! Sherlock? Watson? Get in the back, guys! Hurry!"

As if riding inside a retro sports car was something they did on a daily basis, the corgis leapt onto the passenger seat and immediately took the small 'cargo' space behind the two primary seats. Locking my seatbelt in place as I closed the door, I was about to thank Dottie for her timely intervention when she shifted into first and popped the clutch. With nearly 400 horses under the hood, the 'Vette leapt forward as though it had been shot out of a cannon.

Dottie, it would seem, had become an expert at driving her late mother's sports car.

"Where is he?" Dottie wanted to know. "Do you see him? What does he look like?"

"There he is!" I cried, as I wildly gestured to the right. "Do you see him? He's … watch out! He's doubled back!"

Sure enough, our perp had discovered he was being followed, and had switched directions. Instead of veering off and changing directions, Peter simply reversed course and was now running south on G Street, seemingly straight toward us. After a few moments, I realized what else was in that direction besides the house he had been hiding in. I hastily dialed Vance.

"He's headed for the park!"

"You sound better. Get your second wind?"

"I'm with Dottie. She's driving!"

"Dottie Hanson? That'll work. I'm just approaching Pinetop, and I don't see him. Where is he? Whoa! What the hell? Jeez, someone was in a hurry."

"Dude, that was us! We're in the blue 'Vette!"

"Oh. Are you telling me that he made it by me? How?"

"Who knows? If he makes it to that park, then there's a really good chance he'll get away. That park is huge, and backs up to the forest on the eastern side."

"I'm turning around. Find him, Zack!" The phone went dead.

"Dottie? Stop here. We need to get out."

"Do you see him?" Dottie asked, as she anxiously peered left, then right.

"No, I don't know where he is, but those two? They can find him."

"Ah. Want me to stay close? I can help!"

"Vance is on the way. I owe you lunch, Dottie!"

"I'll be sure to collect! Good luck!"

Unloading the dogs, I was about to tell them what we were here for, but Sherlock and Watson surprised me by immediately pulling me east, deeper into the park. I gave the dogs plenty of slack and encouraged them to run, only they didn't. What was this? What were they doing?

"Come on," I urged. "You can't tell me you don't know where he is. Dogs have a great sense of smell. Sniff him out!"

Both dogs remained motionless, resembling two furry statues. I could barely tell they were breathing. This was new.

A twig snapped loudly nearby. I looked down

at the dogs, expecting them to go tearing off in the direction the noise had come from, only they didn't. Then it became clear what they were doing. They knew Peter was close and neither corgi wanted to alert him that we were nearby.

Hearing a car's engine grow steadily louder, I quickly typed out a message to Vance, telling him to keep driving and don't stop. Peter was hiding nearby and the last thing we wanted was to spook him.

Thankfully, my detective friend got the message and didn't stop his car. The dogs and I watched Vance's beige-colored piece of crap pass and then, noticing how quiet the dogs still were, I dropped to a crouch next to them. Together, we waited to see what Peter was going to do.

I will give the astronomy intern credit. He waited a full ten minutes before he moved. Sherlock and Watson didn't move a muscle the entire time. As for me? Well, I had to maintain that crouch for ten minutes. To say that I was sore was an understatement. I'm surprised my legs and I were still on speaking terms after giving them the order to resume pursuit. Peter had moved off, and I could tell he was trying to be as quiet as possible, but I could still hear him. After all, we were in a forest setting, with needles, broken branches, and acorns strewn about the ground. It was fundamentally impossible to move in any direction without stepping on *something* that would snap underfoot.

Hearing the footsteps start to fade, I gave the

leashes a gentle tug, signaling it was time to go. Sherlock and Watson moved off, but I couldn't help but notice we weren't headed east, but north. Wasn't that the way we had come?

"What the hell is he up to?" I softly wondered aloud. "He's doubled back again?"

Sherlock let out a soft snort, as though he was trying to tell me I was making too much noise. Shrugging, we continued on, choosing our steps with care. And, I must say the dogs led me through the woods without producing so much as a sound. We didn't step on any branches, or dried leaves, or anything..

For the next ten minutes, the dogs and I silently pursued our perp. Yes, Peter stuck to the woods, but it wasn't as bad as you might think. We stayed within sight of G Street the entire time. In fact, I caught sight of Peter several times, squatting next to bushes and fearfully peering out from behind trees. If he was checking to see if he was being followed, and I'm sure he was, then he was totally looking in the wrong direction. Peter, it would seem, thought for certain he was still being pursued by someone in a car.

I watched Peter hide behind yet another tree and, after checking to be certain the coast was clear, he emerged triumphantly from his hiding place. After all, it had been nearly 15 minutes since Vance had driven by. Speaking of Vance, I was honestly surprised he hadn't called. Then again, he also knew I was pursuing Peter, so I'm sure my detective friend didn't want to give me away.

Progress was slow, and I got the impression Peter was making sure no one happened to be following on foot. The dogs and I tracked him north for another few minutes when I realized what he was doing. Pulling out my cell, I fired off a text to Vance.

STILL PURSUING. HE'S HEADING BACK TO G ST HOUSE.

Vance must've been waiting, because I had a response back in less than five seconds.

GOT IT. HEADED BACK NOW. FIGURED HE'D RETURN. PARKED NEARBY.

By the time I made it back to Stephen Carlson's house, Vance was already there. Peter was there, too, and had his hands cuffed behind his back.

"Nicely done!" I praised, as Stephen sullenly let me through the door. I glanced at the homeowner and hooked a thumb in his direction. "What about him?"

"We'll let Captain Nelson decide what to do with him," Vance informed me, as he pulled Peter to his feet. "For the record, Mr. Carlson has been cooperating, so I'm thinking charges will probably not be levied against him."

"What do you think the captain will do?" I asked.

"Ask him yourself. He's on his way here."

"He is? Did he say why?"

"He wants to be certain ET is found and returned to his alma mater. At least, that's my guess."

"Did Peter give you much trouble?"

We both looked at the former intern, who was hanging his head and refused to look either of us in the eye.

"Caught him just as he was coming in the back door. Gave up without a fight."

I looked at the young, twenty-something guy wearing the brown Wookie shirt. He was as skinny as Stephen, had impeccably-styled brown hair, and was still out of breath. The guy did not look healthy at all. I could only assume he spent just as much time outside as his former classmate. And by that, I mean *none.*

"Do I need to call you an ambulance?" Vance cautiously asked. "You're still wheezing pretty bad."

"I'm fine," Peter grumped.

"When was the last time you got some exercise?" I asked.

Peter glared at me for a few moments before dropping his eyes down to the ground again. I watched him look at the dogs and smile briefly.

"I want a lawyer."

"You're going to need it," Vance said. "You stole a nine carat *extraterrestrial* diamond, sport. Then, you hid the thing in a bag of cranberries."

"You then broke into six different grocery

stores," I added, "and did a lot of damage. If you want to help yourself out, then you'd best be letting us know where ET is."

Peter remained tight-lipped and refused to look up from the floor.

"Look, kid," Vance began, "I can't begin to imagine what possessed you to pull this off. Financial troubles or bragging rights, whatever the case may be, you're not good at it."

I noticed Peter's eyes had narrowed. Oh, he was listening, all right.

"*Keep going!*" I silently mouthed to Vance, who nodded.

My friend began ticking off points on his fingers. "You are a terrible lock picker, your diversions were atrocious, and you chose to ditch the merchandise you stole less than a mile from the place where you stole it. What does that tell us? You're no professional, but an amateur."

"I *told* you," Stephen accused, as he looked at his former classmate. "Didn't I tell you that you hadn't thought this through?"

"Shut *up*," Peter grumbled.

"He's not wrong," Vance pointed out. He pushed Peter down onto one of the chairs circling the dinner table. "Come on, kid, 'fess up. Where'd you stash the diamond?"

"I'm not saying anything else without a lawyer being present," Peter insisted.

Right about that time, we heard sirens in the distance. From the sounds of things, the entire PV police force was on their way here. As the wailing of the sirens grew to a level where I had to cover my ears, the dogs stretched out on the linoleum floor, as though they didn't have a care in the world.

"Where is he?" Captain Nelson demanded, as he strode through the door. He and a steady stream of police officers barged through the open door. The captain caught sight of Stephen Carlson, who was about to open his mouth to protest, when a pair of handcuffs were produced. "Do you like jewelry, Mr. Carlson? I'm giving you leniency at the moment. Continue to cooperate, and these might not be in your future."

Stephen hastily nodded. "Yes, sir. Thank you, sir. Please, er, make yourselves comfortable."

The captain approached the dinner table, pulled out a chair, and spun it around. Captain Nelson never broke eye contact as he straddled the chair and clasped his hands in front of him.

"Mr. Peter Grant. We've been looking for you. I hear you have something that doesn't belong to you. Produce this space diamond, the one you stole from the observatory, and I'll try to put in a good word with the district attorney."

"I don't have it," Peter quietly murmured.

"Who does?" Vance asked.

"No one."

"Which means you've hidden it," Vance decided.

Peter shrugged. "It means that I've lost it. I have

no idea where ET is. I thought I could track down the right bag, but evidently, I was wrong. I can only assume someone must have bought the bag before I could get to it."

"And what would you have us believe you've been doing these past couple of days?" Captain Nelson politely inquired. Based on his tone, I could tell the captain wasn't buying any of Peter's explanations.

"I knew I was a person of interest," Peter admitted, using a soft-spoken voice. "I was just trying to lay low, and stay out of the spotlight. I had to figure out what I needed to do next."

"Have you?" Vance demanded.

"Have I *what*?" Peter wanted to know.

"Figured out what you're going to do? That's assuming I believe your story which, for the record, I don't."

Peter shrugged again. "Believe it, don't believe it, I don't care."

I stared at Peter's shirt and suddenly I was smiling. I knew! I actually knew what significance Colin's backpack and those greeting cards at Gary's Grocery had with regard to the case. What could it be, you ask? Well, Colin's backpack had a picture of a very familiar space fighter on it. An X-Wing fighter, if you must know. As most people do know, and myself included, since I'm a huge fan, an X-Wing fighter belongs to the world of *Star Wars*. And the greeting cards? Sherlock and Watson had stopped to stare at them while we were in Gary's Grocery. They were all *Star Wars* themed. And finally, the gardener's boy, the one playing the video game? Well, it just so happened that particular game was an old-fashioned vector game, where you pilot your very own X-Wing fighter as you try to blow up as many TIE-fighters as you can. And finally, our friend Peter, here, is wearing a Chewbacca shirt.

Four separate *Star Wars* references and no one had been able to explain why the dogs had fixated on them. But now? Standing in the living room of this accountant, who was clearly a fan of comic books, and all manner of sci-fi memorabilia, I began to wonder if there was anything from the *Star Wars* universe present. One look was all it took.

I was right. Over there, in the far corner of the living room, on a three-feet tall wooden pedestal, sat the *only Star Wars* collectible that I could see. It was the Lego version of the Millennium Falcon, and before you scoff at that, I can tell you that it's the adult version. Why was it classified for adults? Well, it might have something to do with the fact it has over 7,500 pieces.

Being a *Star Wars* fan myself, I had been drooling over that set for quite some time. However, I just couldn't bring myself to spend $800 for a set of Legos. Sure, it was a huge set, but it was still Legos. So, I'd have to be content with someone else having it and being allowed to put it together.

I also knew, as I slowly approached Han Solo's

beloved space freighter, that the Millennium Falcon was known to be a smuggler's ship, and this particular model incorporated the secret compartments referenced several times in the movies. You couldn't find a better place to hide a cranberry-sized diamond. Well, there was only one way to find out.

"What are you doing?" Stephen demanded. "Don't touch that. It took me nearly 40 hours to put it together!"

"What are you doing, Zack?" Vance wanted to know.

"We're still waiting for the warrant, Mr. Anderson," Captain Nelson informed me.

"I'm a *Star Wars* fan," I told the people seated around the dining table. "I've always wanted to see one of these things up close. You don't mind, do you, Stephen?"

"If you break it, you buy it," the homeowner warned me.

Nodding, I carefully lifted off the back plate of the ship and, in doing so, realized something. Stephen had essentially given me permission to look at his model. That definitely meant he was not in cahoots with Peter, seeing how the poor intern had a look of horror on his face and appeared as though he was ready to puke. Setting the back plate safely off to the side, I took my first look at the guts of the ship. Wow. I used to think these Lego kits were for only kids, but the level of detail in this one? It could only be for an adult. I could see the storage hold, the little seating area where Chewie and Luke played that weird space chess, and there, in the hallway, were the fake panels I knew were hiding the secret compartments.

Lifting the small cover plates out of the way, I leaned in to take a closer look at the newly revealed space. I grinned as I saw what was concealed within. Vance appeared next to me and handed me a pair of latex gloves. Properly protected, I bent down to retrieve the object that had been stashed inside the ship: the extraterrestrial diamond!

Holding the glittering diamond aloft, I victoriously turned around and approached the table. That's when we all heard Peter let out a collective groan. Stephen let out a comical squawk of surprise before he turned to his former classmate and threw a right hook.

He missed, which resulted in him spinning around and plopping unceremoniously onto the floor. Vance, doing an admirable job of keeping a straight face, gave Stephen a hand up before turning to Peter.

"I hope it was worth it, pal."

ELEVEN

T here is nothing I like more than the smell of a turkey cooking for the better part of the day."

"If I cooked this bird for the better part of the day, then we'd end up trying to eat a charcoal briquette. That's the most common mistake people make on Thanksgiving."

"Overcooking the bird," I said, nodding. "Makes sense, I suppose."

Jillian smiled at me. "Has it ever happened to you?"

"On many an occasion," I recalled. "My father actually decided to give my mother a break one year. He wanted her to be able to relax, so he bought a turkey fryer."

"That's definitely not the healthy way to go," Jillian lamented.

"I would agree. Especially since Dad sat down to watch a football game and promptly forgot about it."

Jillian covered her mouth. "Oh, no! What happened?"

"Easy. We ended up eating turkey jerky that year."

"Oh, you and your stories," Jillian laughed.

I shrugged. "I have been known to bend the truth here and there, but on this particular occasion, it was true. At least the parts that were still edible tasted pretty good. Hey, do we have a final head count yet? People will start arriving soon, and I need to make certain we have enough chairs."

Jillian nodded. "There's you and me, Hannah and Colin, Lisa and Kimmi, Taylor, and Dottie."

I paused as a thought occurred. "Do you mean to tell me that the only other male will be Colin?"

Jillian batted her eyes at me. "I suppose so. Will that be a problem?"

"I guess not. I mean, I am planning on decimating the poor boy on Robotron."

Less than an hour later, Carnation Cottage was full of bustling activity. Thankfully, Jillian had a huge kitchen in her house, so three extra sets of hands didn't result in people getting in each other's way. Kimmi and I wisely decided to stay out of everyone's way and elected to sit at the breakfast bar, where we could watch the activity. Turning to the young Asian girl, I gave her a smile.

"So, Kimmi, what type of work do you do?"

"I'm a Realtor. Back in Honolulu, I was a bartender for a local cruise line. What do you do, Mr. Anderson? Besides making your own wine, that is?"

Lisa Martinez looked up from the cutting board where she had been peeling carrots and chopping celery, shaking her head.

"K? Did you just ask Zack what type of work he does?"

Kimmi nodded. "Well, yeah. He asked me what I do, so I thought I'd ask him. Is there something wrong?"

"What was the name of the book you just read?" Lisa off-handedly asked.

"*Misty Moors*. Why? Would you like to borrow my copy?"

Lisa pointed at me and grinned. Surprised, Kimmi turned to regard me with a skeptical look.

"Would *you* like to borrow it? I mean, I know it's probably not your thing, but ..."

"For heaven's sake, K," Lisa interrupted. "He wrote it!"

Kimmi's eyes widened. "Impossible. My book was written by a woman."

I gave the confused girl a mock-bow. "Ms. Chastity Wadsworth, at your service."

Kimmi's face blushed bright red. "You? You wrote my book? But ... but that's not possible!"

"You really need to pay attention to me more often," Lisa chuckled. She noticed a few strands of her jet-black hair had fallen out of her ponytail, and promptly pulled her hair loose to redo her ponytail. "I told you he's a world-famous author. I also told you he works with the police."

Kimmi automatically looked out, toward the living room. Colin was there, playing with Sherlock and Watson.

"The dogs! Oh, I remember now. You solve crimes with the dogs, don't you?"

"Guilty as charged," I admitted. "Tell me, how have you been enjoying PV so far?"

"I love it here," Kimmi gushed. "The only complaint I have is that there's no shoreline, no water, and no surfing. I miss getting my feet wet."

"Rascal River is out there," I reminded the girl. "The water might be a tad colder than you'd like, but ..."

"A tad?" Kimmi interrupted, laughing. "The last time I stuck a toe in that river water, I had an ice cube attached to it when I pulled it out. No, thank you. You guys can keep your freakishly cold water."

There was a knock at the door, which set both of the dogs off. However, I recognized that particular bark. It wasn't an agitated bark, but an excited member-of-the-pack-was-home type of bark. Looking around the room, I realized it could only be one person.

"Hi, Taylor! Hey, let me get that for you."

The woman with the short, curly blond hair stepped inside, gave me a hug once her hands were free of the heavy platter she had been holding, and then dropped down to the ground so she could greet the corgis.

"If it isn't the smartest doggies in the whole,

wide world!"

Sherlock and Watson were ecstatic. They were running circles around Taylor, all while barking maniacally. Thankfully, the greeting only lasted a few moments before both dogs settled down and promptly flopped onto their backs. Taylor laughed and gave each of them a belly rub.

Jillian appeared next to her friend and smiled. "Taylor! So very nice to see you! Wow, something smells fantastic! What's on the tray?"

"It's my own version of a honey-baked ham, although I think mine's better. Then again, I could be biased."

"Ooo, I'm so glad calories don't count today," I exclaimed.

Every other person in the house, with the exception of Colin, regarded me with a piteous look. Before anyone could speak, however, I waggled a finger.

"Don't you dare. Everyone knows calories aren't counted on holidays. Now, everyone, repeat after me: calories don't count on Thanksgiving."

"Calories don't count on Thanksgiving," six women intoned, giggling profusely as they did.

"I'm *so* adopting that rule," Dottie announced, as she mixed something together in a small bowl.

"What are you making?" I asked.

The new proprietor of A Lazy Afternoon held up a spatula covered with a yellow substance. "Deviled eggs. I've got to make sure the filling is just right."

"I love deviled eggs," I said.

"Bet you're gonna love the recipe I made for today," Kimmi said.

I looked back at Lisa's girlfriend. "Oh? I don't know. I can be pretty picky."

Six women all snorted, at the same time.

"I'm gonna choose to ignore that," I said, with a grin. "Okay, Kimmi, hit me with your best. What did you bring?"

"Bubble bread."

I shrugged. "I like bread, and as long as it doesn't have raisins in it, or walnuts, I'm pretty sure I'll like it."

"I said you're going to *love* this bread," Kimmi clarified.

Intrigued, I looked at the person sitting next to me. "All right, woman. You have my attention."

Kimmi laughed. "The more you talk, the more I can hear your voice in your books. Now, as for bubble bread, it's also been called monkey bread."

"Prithee, continue," I drawled, which made Kimmi laugh again and Jillian giggle.

"You place uncooked, unrisen dinner rolls into a greased Bundt pan. Add some cinnamon and brown sugar. Then, you take a package of instant butterscotch pudding and sprinkle that over the whole thing. Then, bake it in the oven. The rolls will rise and everything kinda melts together. Oh, it's to die for. Here, let me help you with that."

"Huh?' I stammered, but before I knew what she was doing, Kimmi was dabbing at the corners of my mouth with a napkin.

"You're drooling, Zack."

"Oh, hardy har har. Umm, did you get it all?"

The ladies laughed again.

Dinner was fantastic. I never knew turkey could be so moist and flavorful. Growing up, I had gotten used to needing some type of condiment in order to get the turkey down. I'm ashamed to say it was usually ketchup. Jillian, though, introduced me to a whole new world of flavors. Sure, there were still things I wasn't a fan of, but stuffing? Holy cow, I loved it.

As a kid, I avoided just about everything at the Thanksgiving table. Everyone called me 'picky', or a 'bottom feeder', but I honestly think it was because my mother wasn't the best cook. Don't get me wrong, she had some recipes that were fantastic, but it wasn't until many years later that I realized pork chops weren't supposed to bounce off the floors. They could actually be moist and flavorful, and *not* become a dehydrated strip of protein.

But, I digress. We were here, sitting together, and enjoying each other's dishes. I was well into my second plate of turkey and ham when Dottie brought up the inevitable.

"Zack? Were you able to catch the guy I helped you chase?"

The chatter at the table came to a standstill.

"Yeah, actually, we did," I reported. "Turns out he wasn't the sharpest tool in the shed."

Dottie slapped a hand over her mouth and giggled. "What makes you say that?"

"He thought he'd give us the slip by sneaking back to the rock where he had been hiding, and the only thing he did to lose us was to duck behind trees. Sherlock and Watson, understandably, were up to the task of following him."

"What happened?" Lisa curiously asked.

"I got word to Vance, and he managed to get back to the house before Peter did. Peter was arrested the moment he snuck in the back door."

"Good," Taylor decided. "Serves him right."

"He was a good kid who made some bad decisions," I announced, as I helped myself to a few more of Hannah's butt rolls. And yeah, I know how that sounds. In case you've forgotten why they have that name, Google them. You'll see. "Honestly? I feel bad for the guy."

"Pretend I don't know anything about the case," Kimmi began. "What did this guy do?"

Lisa was shaking her head. "Seriously, K, you need to pull your nose out of your book more. There's a whole world out there, waiting to be discovered."

"Ignore her," I said. "On behalf of Ms. Wadsworth, we appreciate the patronage."

Kimmi slipped her arm through mine and stuck her tongue out at Lisa. "Why thank you, kind sir."

"To answer your question," I began, "Peter Grant was working at an observatory, up in Washington State. They were studying a special extra-terrestrial diamond called 'ET'."

"Extraterrestrial?" Kimmi repeated, and she frowned. "What does that mean? It came from space?"

I nodded. "Exactly. It caught a ride with a meteorite on the way down. Peter Grant, the intern in question, had been assisting a team who had been studying meteorites. Scientists, right? I personally think they're some of the smartest people out there, but in this case, they goofed. They made the mistake of leaving one of their interns alone with it. Unsupervised."

"And he couldn't resist the temptation," Lisa added.

"Sherlock and Watson found it," Hannah added.

I grinned and pointed at Colin. "Actually, Colin helped me find it."

The boy looked up, with half a roll shoved in his mouth. "I did?"

"Colin!" Hannah scolded. "Don't speak with your mouth full!"

"Sorry." A few moments passed while Colin furiously chewed his roll. Once his mouth was clear, he looked up at me. "I helped you find the stolen diamond?"

I nodded. "A few days ago, you were wearing a backpack in your mother's shop. Do you remember which one it was?"

The boy nodded. "Yes. I only have the one."

"What about the backpack?" Taylor wanted to know.

"Tell them what's on it," I instructed.

Colin shrugged. "Master Yoda."

"Master *who*?" Kimmi asked, puzzled.

"You need to take her out more," I chortled, as I addressed Lisa.

Kimmi smiled and looked triumphantly at her significant other. "You heard him!"

"Master Yoda," I slowly explained, "is the Jedi Master who trained countless people in the ways of … all right. I'm going to stop right there. If I didn't sound like a dork before, then I sure as hell do now. Umm, long story short, Colin's backpack captured Sherlock and Watson's interest, only I didn't know why."

"Until now," Dottie guessed.

I nodded. "*Star Wars*. There were several un-explained *Star Wars* references. Greeting cards at one of the burglarized stores, a video game being played by the gardener's son, and finally, the shirt Peter was wearing when we found him."

"What was he wearing?" Jillian asked.

"A Chewbacca shirt. Somehow, I had to find the part that everyone's favorite sci-fi franchise played with this case. There, in the classmate's living room, was the answer: an iconic spaceship, made out of Legos."

"The Millennium Falcon?" Colin asked.

I held up a hand and waited for Colin to give me a high-five. "Exactamundo. Anyone who is a fan of *Star Wars* will know that the Millennium Falcon is a smuggler's ship. It has secret storage compartments. Suddenly, I knew where Peter must've stashed the diamond. Sure enough, I was right."

"Brilliant!" Colin beamed.

Kimmi raised a hand. "Just tell me what's the deal with all the cranberries. Why was this diamond thief fixated on cranberries?"

"There was a cranberry processing plant next door to the observatory," Jillian explained. "When Peter realized he needed a way to smuggle the diamond out of the state, he headed next door. His roommate's girlfriend worked in shipping, so he dropped the diamond in a passing bag and then noted where the bags were due to be shipped. In this case, that batch was slated to be delivered to MDC, which stands for Medford Distribution Center. However, Peter couldn't find the right bag."

"That's why he kept hitting different grocery stores," I added. "He somehow duped MDC into giving him a list of their customers, and before you can say cranberry juice, small grocery stores began noticing some unwanted attention."

"I'm just glad no one was hurt," Jillian decided. She reached for her glass of wine, which had me reaching for my glass of sparkling cider. "Everyone? I'd like to make a toast."

Everyone reached for their drinks. Hannah nudged her son and inclined her head toward his chocolate milk. After a few moments, everyone had their drinks in their hands and held aloft.

"To family, friends, and a wonderful year. To my handsome fiancé, Zachary, and his two precious dogs, Sherlock and Watson. I don't think I could feel more blessed, even if I tried. Happy Thanksgiving, everyone!"

I have been asked repetitively whether or not I was going to include COVID-19 in the books. I know of some authors who have done so, and found myself seriously considering it. After all, it's as real as you can get, and regardless what certain people are saying, it isn't a hoax. It's nasty business.

So, with that being said, I decided to include a few references. The scene with Zack and Jillian experiencing the woes of trying to do some normal grocery shopping, when there were those intent on hoarding every darn thing they could get their hands on, was based on real events. I wish I could say it wasn't, but I wanted to vent my frustration about the way this particular pandemic has been handled. As I write this, the national election is one week away. I typically won't indulge in politics, nor will I force my opinion and beliefs on others. However, if ever there was a time to make your voice heard, it'd be now, so I hope all you fellow Americans cast your ballot and voted.

For anyone familiar with the Jacobsen Observatory, I first want to say that, yes, I did take a few liberties with the telescope. There's a 6" telescope on the premises, but figuring it was kinda small, I increased it to a 15". If you've used the observatory, or have taken offense to that, sorry!

I've got the next three Corgi Case Files planned out. Well, planned out in my head, actually. The next will be written during the month of November, where I will, once again, participate in the NaNoWriMo challenge. What's the title going to be called? Case of the Shady Shamrock (Corgi Case Files #12). I'm recommending to my publisher that it be released in February, so that they can market it for St. Patty's Day. I've written a number of holiday-themed books now, so it's nice to include a new holiday this time around. What's the story about? Let's just say a mysterious chest appears on Zack's doorstep. Who sent it? What does it contain? And why are there people after it?

My lips are sealed.

One final note. I'd like to resume doing something that I started a while ago, and that's to give a few recommendations. If you've finished this story, and are hungry for more, then I have a few choices for you. I heartily recommend you check out:

Connie Shelton's Charlie Parker series
CJ Love's Shakespearean Murder Mysteries
J.H. Sked's Blue Moon Detectives series

For those of you who would like to make sure they never miss a release, or would like to be notified whenever I'm hosting a book giveaway, please sign up for my newsletter, which can be found on my website, listed below.

And finally, an appeal. If you enjoyed this story,

please consider leaving it a review at the retailer where you purchased it. Reviews are an author's best friend.

Happy reading!

J.

www.AuthorJMPoole.com

October, 2020

THE CORGI CASE FILES SERIES

Zack and the corgis will return, in Case of the Shady Shamrock! A mysterious chest appears on Zack's doorstep. Who sent it? What does it contain? And why are there people after it? Watch for this new adventure in February 2021

Sign up for Jeffrey's newsletter on his website to get all the latest corgi news: **www.AuthorJMPoole.com**

Have you missed any of the Corgi Case Files?
Available in e-book and paperback

Case of the One-Eyed Tiger
Case of the Fleet-Footed Mummy
Case of the Holiday Hijinks
Case of the Pilfered Pooches
Case of the Muffin Murders
Case of the Chatty Roadrunner
Case of the Highland House Haunting
Case of the Ostentatious Otters
Case of the Dysfunctional Daredevils
Case of the Abandoned Bones
Case of the Great Cranberry Caper

If you enjoy Epic Fantasy, check out Jeff's other series:
Pirates of Perz
Tales of Lentari
Bakkian Chronicles

Made in the USA
Las Vegas, NV
31 January 2022